The Gravity Box

Adventures of the Two Most Powerful
Kids in the Universe.

A Novel by
Norman Macera

Original Copyright 1986.
Date of publishing 2020

ISBN: 978-0-578-67683-8

The Gravity Box was originally written and copyrighted in 1986, but life sent me off in other directions. Bringing it out, and reading it again, was an adventure almost as great as those facing our main characters.

Special Thanks To:

Veronica Kegal Giglio, for all her help, and championing of my work and me.

Hector Ortega, for his great encouragement, and wonderful cover design.

Craig Walker, for his incredible friendship, and all his help in pulling this book together.

Cass Macera, best Mom in the World, for her endless love and support over the years.

This story of two great friends is dedicated to the truly greatest friend in the Universe.

Dennis Sigmund

Love ya' buddy.

Table of Contents

PART I. AN UNWANTED TRIP TO THE MOON 1

CHAPTER 1. GONERS FOR GOOD...1

CHAPTER 2. HOW WE MET THE PROFESSOR AND JUNK LIKE THAT 10

CHAPTER 3. THE LAST SECRET.. 16

CHAPTER 4. THE MISSION.. 33

CHAPTER 5. UP, UP AND AWAY 39

CHAPTER 6. HIDE AND SEEK IN THE SKY 53

PART II. THE BAD GUYS IN BLACK.. 71

CHAPTER 1. WHAT HAPPENED WHEN WE GOT BACK HOME.. 71

CHAPTER 2. THE PLAN 78

CHAPTER 3. HOW WE BECAME THE INVISIBLE MEN 86

CHAPTER 4. THE RAID 91

CHAPTER 5. WHEN IT LOOKED LIKE THE END OF THE ROAD 103

CHAPTER 6. THE CHASE 109

CHAPTER 7. DANGER IN THE WOODS 117

CHAPTER 8. RESCUE AT THE LAB. 127

CHAPTER 9. WHAT WOULD JAMES BOND DO?................. 137

CHAPTER 10. WHEN DANGER REALLY BECAME OUR BUSINESS.. 151

CHAPTER 11. THE GREAT ESCAPE.................................... 165

CHAPTER 12. STALKING THE STALKERS............................ 179

CHAPTER 13. THE CLOUD GAME...................................... 189

CHAPTER 14. THE MAN OF STEEL AT THE O.K. CORRAL 201

CHAPTER 15. THE WHOLE TRUTH AND NOTHING BUT... 215

CHAPTER 16. DID WE REALLY THINK IT'D WORK?..........231

CHAPTER 17. A BOY'S GOTTA DO, WHAT A BOY'S GOTTA DO 247

EPPI-LOG...265

PART I. AN UNWANTED TRIP TO THE MOON

CHAPTER 1. GONERS FOR GOOD

Guess I always knew that people could fly. Don't ask me how I knew, I just did. Maybe it was 'cause I could fly in my dreams, or maybe it was, like my Dad would say, I had an overactive imagination. And as I was floating higher and higher toward the clouds, I was beginning to wish that I had been wrong, and wanted to be stuck back on the ground with everybody else. There was another thing; I began to feel really sorry for stealing the Gravity Box. Actually, I hadn't started out to steal it. It was just like being taken for a long joy ride. I mean I'd already been given permission to take it, only not for such a long time. There was only one problem with that, I didn't know how to turn the darn thing off. So, along with wishing that I had never learned to fly, I was sorry I'd been so selfish. So there I was climbing closer to the stars, and if my memory of science class was right, I would be running out of air very soon. It was already getting very cold way up there.

Don't have to tell you I was scared. Who wouldn't be? And all that stuff they tell you about your life flashing in front of you, not true! All I could see before me was a big white cloud that I was about to pass through, and the ground seeming like a million miles away.

Guess you'd call it a gravity machine, though it was more like a box. It didn't have any clinking parts or wheels, nothing that moved; so, I didn't think it was a machine at all. What it was, was a black box, with a hole in the front covered with glass. Even so, I still couldn't see what was inside, or what made it tick. On the sides were two bars sticking out, a lot like handlebars on a motorcycle. Guess I should've let go of the handles a thousand feet before, but it was too late to think of that way up in the sky. Strange thing was, that once you grabbed hold of those handles, it was like you were doing the flying yourself, not just being pulled up in the air by the box.

Passing through the cloud was really like passing through nothing at all. It didn't seem to have anything to it. It just seemed to be a reminder of how high I had gone, and what a mess I had gotten myself into.

The stars shined brighter then I had ever seen them before. They glimmered brighter and brighter, as I seemed to be drifting dangerously close to them. I knew that I would burn up way before I actually got to a star. I'd probably get fried by the closest star along the way. That would be the Sun. Not that that should be any worry of mine, the air would run out years before that could ever happen. That didn't make me feel any better about all of this. Another thing bothering me, once my air ran out, I'd probably let go of the box, and fall back to earth. So I was running scared from a lot of different directions, with nowhere really to run to.

Like I said, I was scared out of my mind. Think that was the problem. I had gotten so darn scared, I forgot everything the Professor had taught us about the Gravity Box. Then a funny thing happened. I began to forget all about my problems, maybe it was the air getting thin, or who knows what; but for whatever reason I began to think about my Mom, and Dad, and even my little sister, who most of the time I can't stand. Yet there they were inside my head like a moving picture, with them all watching television, and snacking on popcorn and soda pop. Can't remember what we were watching, but whatever it was, I was real happy to be there with them.

From there everything went blank, like a big black cloud had covered up the movie screen inside my head. Guess that was the air disappearing around me. When the big black cloud was gone, I was in Professor Burkhardt's laboratory, with him waving a hanky over my head. When he saw my eyes fluttering, he started right in on me.

"You bad, bad boy! You could have been killed, could've died, my heart could have stopped!"

I could tell just by looking at him that he was a nervous wreck. Standing with him was Jimmy. He was the smart one. My friend I mean. He had gotten me through most of my math and science classes. Could tell from the look on his face that he was mad at me too.

"That was stupid man," Jimmy yelled at me, and he was right.

Trying to get up I found myself feeling heavy, like there was a ton of metal filling the inside of my arms and chest.

"Lay down," said the Professor, "don't try and get up yet." My body didn't want to move anyway, so I knew that he was right. So that was no problem.

"Stupid man, really stupid!" I knew that Jimmy was gonna be harping on me all night long. "We'd better get back home before we get in more trouble," he warned me.

I tried to get up again, and this time it was easier, not real easy though.

"How'd I get back," I asked kinda curious like.

"You are a bad, bad boy," the Professor started in again. When he saw me take a deep breath and hold it, he stopped. He could tell that my head was aching, and that there would be plenty of time to holler at me later.

"Okay, go home," he said, "and don't come back unless you are going to be a good boy!"

"I'll take care of him," Jimmy told the Professor, like he was taking care of a little kid or something.

Then he helped me off of the laboratory table, and onto the floor. My legs felt a little wobbly, but I could walk all right. When I got to the door, I was beginning to feel like a real jerk; so I turned back and gave the Professor; "Sorry, it was really dumb."

He just waved me off, and went back to his work, but Jimmy slammed right into me with a: "It wasn't just dumb, that was the stupidest thing I've ever seen."

Stepping outside I said, "cut me a break, will ya'," it was dumb, I knew that, but a kid had to defend himself, especially from the truth that he had been a big idiot.

And then Jimmy got quiet. It was night, and since the lab was in the middle of the woods, practically, it was as dark as anything out there. There weren't any other houses for at least a mile, and with only the moon in the sky there wasn't much light to go by. We both knew the way pretty well, so there wasn't much problem there.

"How'd I get down," I tried again, asking Jimmy.

"Look Shawn," he said, his voice still sounded a bit angry. "I wasn't too happy about tonight, I'm not really that good with the gravity machine yet..."

"You mean you did it?" He didn't answer; he just dropped his head, and continued to walk. "Thanks man," I said it, and I meant it. Jimmy was a good friend, maybe better than I deserved, but I wasn't gonna go that far, and tell him that.

A few more steps, then he stopped, and turned to me again. When he spoke to me this time, his voice wasn't mad anymore. It was sort of sincere like.

"You know I'm glad I did it." This time I didn't answer. "But," and that "but" meant that he was gonna talk to me like he was my Dad or something, and I hated when he did that: "Nobody's supposed to know about the gravity machine yet. You know it's a big secret, and if somebody had seen you..."

"Alright, I know, I know, it won't happen again."

"Okay," he said, and we started to go on once more. We didn't get much further, when Jimmy stopped me, sudden like, with a quick grab at my arm.

"What are you trying to..."

"Shhh," he put his finger to his lips. He had almost scared me half to death.

"What's wrong?"

"Shhh," he came again, and this time he put his hand over my mouth, to make sure I'd listen.

At that instant we both stood there, quiet, in the dark, waiting for what, I didn't know. For a moment it seemed like there was nobody else in the world, and then I heard it, a cracking sound, like somebody stepping over fallen twigs.

"What's that," I asked, only this time I whispered

"I don't know," Jimmy whispered back.

"Maybe a deer, or something."

"Maybe. Just stay still for a minute." And we did. We listened for the longest time. For a while there was nothing, and then more crunching sounds, a lot more. Whatever it was had to be big, I thought, and seemed to be moving our way.

"It's comin' this..."

There was another "shhh," from Jimmy, who then pushed me behind a huge tree to wait for whatever.

"I don't like this," I whispered, but Jimmy did not answer, he just kept peeking from behind the tree. As the noise grew louder, I felt like I wanted to run, but Jimmy stayed there, so I did too. Look, the guy had just saved my life about an hour before; so I couldn't leave him, which seemed like it would be the smart thing to do. Then it came, or should I say they came. Four, of what looked to be shadow creatures, all dark, all man size, and all very, very scary. I gasped. I didn't want to, it just come out. Then I saw Jimmy's head turn, I couldn't see the look on his face, but I could only guess that it wasn't smiling. Funny, that when the shadow creatures reached the road coming close to the house, all of their footsteps stopped making noise.

We watched a little longer, soon they were at the side of the Professor's lab. The lab was part of the house, which the old man lived in, and was on the ground floor. Suddenly we knew what the shadow creatures were, as one glided in front of the light that was coming out of the window, we could see that they were really men. Just plain, ordinary men dressed in all black track suits, with hoods over their heads. Somehow, that didn't make me any less scared.

Jimmy whispered, "Let's get closer."

"What," I couldn't believe he had actually said that.

"Let's see what they're up to."

"Are you nuts," maybe I was the smart one after all.

"You don't want anything to happen to the Professor, do you?"

"Well…" I was trying to think of an answer, because I didn't want anything to happen to me either. There wasn't any chance to think about it, because Jimmy gave me a "let's go," and a tug on my shoulder, and we were on our way down to see what the men in the dark clothes were up to.

All that ran through my mind as we got closer to the house and to the men; was what good is a twelve-year-old coward gonna be against four big men. You see Jimmy never thought about things like that, but Shawn Malloy's mother didn't raise no fool. Okay, maybe that trip through the clouds wasn't the brightest thing in the world, but I hardly ever got that stupid twice in one night. Slowly we moved toward the house, and the dark strangers that were spying through the window of the old professor's laboratory. Each step taken sent the sound of snapping twigs to my ears, and shivers down my spine. How

7

did those men become so quiet as they neared the lab? All at once Jimmy put a palm in my chest, stopping me right in my tracks.

"Close enough," he said in a low voice. I wasn't complaining. Now we just stood and watched. What we were watching, I wasn't exactly sure. Two men stayed low, duck walking just under the window. The other two seemed to be doing something to the telephone wires that went into the house. One of the men by the window removed what looked like a small box from underneath his shirt. Carefully he stood up, and sneaked a peak inside the lab. He waited for just about a minute, and then he raised the box to the level of the window. Thinking it must have been a camera, 'cause I thought I heard a clicking sound, and then he ducked down again. Right after that, the other two men came back to the side of the window. Without saying a word, the one man, guess he was the boss, motioned to the others, and they were all moving away from the house again, without making a sound, and headed right back in our direction. That wasn't good.

"Jeez…" I felt my stomach get all tight.

Jimmy didn't say anything; he just pushed me behind another tree. For a moment the men stopped, as if they had heard something. All I could hear was my heart pounding inside my chest, boom, boom, boom, like it was gonna explode, and I was actually afraid that they were gonna hear it thumping like a herd of wild buffalo stampeding. Then they moved on. Maybe they thought what they heard was a deer or something. The men passed only inches away from us. I don't think I've ever held my breath that long before. Then they were gone.

"What the heck was all that?"

"Shhh…" Jimmy told me, and we listened. From far away you could hear the motor of a car engine, and then the sound faded.

"We'd better tell the Professor," I said to Jimmy.

"No," he said.

"Why not," I really didn't understand why we wouldn't be racing off to tell the Professor what had just happened.

"Because, those guys just bugged the Professor's place. Or least I think that's what they did. If we tell the Professor they'll know, I think."

"But..."

"Then they'll know we know. Tomorrow," he said, "we'll think of something tomorrow."

We were going home, and I was never gonna be so happy to see anything in my life. Even though we were gonna be in big trouble when we got there, but that's another story.

CHAPTER 2. HOW WE MET THE PROFESSOR AND JUNK LIKE THAT

Guess I ought to tell you how we met Professor Burkhardt. Well, it wasn't me who met him first, it was Jimmy. You see Jimmy's a scientist. Well not really, but he thinks he is. He's always getting into trouble making messes, and trying to fix junk, and a couple times he's nearly blown up his own house. Don't get me wrong, Jimmy's a smart kid, and lot's a times his stuff really works, but most of the times, it just gets him into big trouble. By him, I mean we, 'cause, somehow he always manages to drag me in on it. Might call me his guinea pig, or partner in crime. I think I like being called partner in crime better. Whatever, it's usually bad news when Jimmy calls up for a test run on one of his latest inventions. Anyway, Jimmy's my best friend, so if I'm gonna get in trouble, I'm glad it's with him.

Actually, it was Jimmy's newest invention that made us run into the Professor. I mean really run into him. Here's how it worked. Me and him, the both of us, asked our parents for briefcases to carry our books in, instead of the usual school bags all the other guys had. Our parents already think we're crazy, so they didn't make a big deal out of it, and we got the cases. Jimmy's idea was to put two metal slides with some Crazy Glue onto one side of the case. This was to be hidden by a nameplate that was to be taped over it. Inside the briefcase, and tucked under our lunch and all the other stuff was a flat piece of steel with ball bearing wheels attached. So, what would happen, if we ever had to make a fast break for it, like mobsters we're chasing us? Well, that never actually happened, but Jimmy thought that it didn't hurt to be prepared. Anyway, all you'd have to do is to rip off the nameplate, slide the wheels into the metal groves, and skate off on top of the briefcase. Supposed to work just like a regular skateboard. We were both great skaters, me being the best, so it was the perfect escape vehicle for when a Chinese warlord dropped into the neighborhood. That kinda never happened either.

Sounds a little strange, but Jimmy could be scientist one minute, and James Bond the next. James Bond was a super spy in movies and books. When Jimmy got tired of being a super scientist, he wanted to be a super spy, just like his hero James Bond. Spy was another game we'd love to play. Jimmy had all these crazy gadgets for fighting crime, and most of them worked. What's the good of having all that brainpower, if you can't take on the bad guys, and save the world? Like, we were the only kids around our way with safety parachutes on our ten speeds, in case the brakes didn't work, or we were going off a cliff or something. The best was the exploding bottle cap gun, but let me get back to the Professor.

We were having a secret testing back in the woods for the new briefcase device. It was a code red, top priority mission, so nobody was supposed to see us. I mean what good is having a secret escape briefcase, if everybody knows about it? So anyway, we were looking for a piece of ground that's hard enough, so that the wheels didn't sink in, but private enough that nobody would catch us in our code red, high security testing. Let me tell you, in the dirt, this invention was not too great. It worked, but it was a bumpy ride. Me being the better skater could ride the dirt a little better than Jimmy, but still not great. But we kept looking for a nice, private spot to make our secret testing ground. We were going nowhere plenty fast. Jimmy was really down about it. Then I got a brilliant idea. I told him, that we should go over to Dead Man's Hill. That was nothing more than a large slope, that if you drove off of it you'd probably get killed. Nobody ever did, but that's another story.

Dead Man's Hill was on the edge of an old paint factory, with a huge flat tar parking lot, that dipped right off into the large drop. It was near six o'clock, and everybody had probably gone home. The parking lot was perfect for scientific testing, and skate boarding. We made it there in about fifteen, twenty minutes.

"This is perfect Shawn," he said.

"Hey, I got some brains myself."

"Some," he said but, I wasn't sure he meant it "We'd better hurry."

The sun was going down fast, and the little bit of it that was lighting the sky wasn't going to be around for long.

Right away we set up the skates. They slid easily into the metal grooves. We put them on the ground, and the next thing I knew we were gliding all over the place. Me better than Jimmy, 'cause I'm a better skater. I think I told ya' that already. I'm not bragging, it's just true. He was the one with the brains, but I could out skate him. In fact, I was better on bikes, football, all that kinda stuff. The only thing Jimmy did better than me was thinking. Anyway, he didn't mind too much, 'cause he was so happy about riding his invention. It was so neat being the only ones in the world with: Special

Counterintelligence Mobile Units. That's what he called them, and I guess he should know, 'cause he invented them. The wind was whizzing by us, and it felt so cool just riding the briefcases, that we both started laughing. We both started at the same time, out of nowhere.

An extra hard kick off of the ground would send you zooming along. We were shouting and hollering like two nuts, just missing each other as we raced back and forth across the parking lot. Then I guess we got a little careless. It was me really, because I started playing daredevil, coasting real close to the edge of the hill, and then swerving at the last minute. I mean, what else were you supposed to do on Dead Man's Hill? Jimmy told me not to be stupid, and the more he told me, the stupider I got. I guess I was trying to teach him a lesson. Funny thing, every time I tried to teach him a lesson, I ended up getting one myself.

"You're gonna break your neck, dummy," he yelled.

And at that moment, I'd twist my hips around; the briefcase would pivot in the opposite direction, and come sailing back at him.

"Very funny," he said.

The next time I decided to really give him a scare. I picked up my speed with three or four good pushes off of the ground.

"Shawn," I heard his voice call to me. I just kept laughing as I picked up speed, then I noticed that I was going a bit too fast, so my foot hit the ground as I went to turn. It was almost dark, so I'm not sure if I hit sand or what, but my foot wasn't working right, and I swear, I thought I was going to be the first one to actually get killed on Dead Man's Hill. As the briefcase began to fly off of the side of

13

the hill, I was going along with it. Jimmy was right behind me. Didn't notice that then, but I'm telling you now so you understand what happened next. He saw my problem right away, and was already on the way to the rescue. Jimmy was good that way, always there for back up. Guess it was my screaming as I soared through the air that got him moving.

"Shawn," he yelled again, but Shawn had already gone over the embankment. My luck, the briefcase had gotten away from me. Hitting the dirt hard, I began to roll. Have to tell you, screamed all the time I was bouncing, and falling down Dead Man's Hill. Jimmy tried to stop too, but he must have found the same patch of sand. Only he must have decided to ride his briefcase to the bottom, because a second later him and the case came soaring out and over the edge, like he was some kinda mountain skier. I caught only a second of the look on his face as he passed over me, and I could tell that he wasn't happy. His yell echoed off on the surrounding rocks, as he continued the ride the briefcase like a born surfer. Didn't think he had it in him. In no time, I was following him down, but he was going too fast to keep up with.

"Fall off, fall off," I called to him, but he was going too fast, and beginning to move faster all the time. The wheels must have hit a rock, and slid out from of the metal grooves that held them in place. Jimmy was now using only the slick surface of the briefcase itself to ride to the bottom. It looked great, and if he hadn't been terrified, I'm sure he would have found it very exciting.

Near to the bottom, the case glided across a flat rock that sent good old Jimmy sailing out over some other rocks. His scream sounded like pure terror as he became airborne again. I closed my eyes for that. When I opened them, he was gone, out of sight. As quick as possible, I made my way down to the bottom of the hill.

"Jimmy, Jimmy", I called, but there was no answer. Going fast, and trying not to trip over the rocks or anything, I got to the flat ground below. "Jimmy," I yelled one more time

"Hurry up," I heard his voice.

"You all right?"

"Get over here, will you," he sounded really scared.

It was getting darker, and a lot harder to see, but following his voice got me there.

"You all right," I kept calling over this really big rock. Then I saw him. "Who's that?"

"Whoever he is, he's the victim of an unidentified flying briefcase."

There they were, Jimmy on the ground, and being crushed by some strange old man in some white get up. Oh by the way, that guy was Professor Burkhardt.

CHAPTER 3. THE LAST SECRET

Both Jimmy and I just looked at each other. For a minute, neither of us knew exactly what to do. Then, out of nowhere, the old guy moans. Scared us at first, but then we were both just glad that he was still alive.

"Come on," Jimmy cried out, "help get him off of me."

Right away I jumped down off of the rock, and landed beside the both of them. The guy was shaking his head, and mumbling something to himself when he noticed Jimmy being crushed under him. For the first time I saw his face. He had no hair on the top of his head; on the sides he had short hair, with a little gray mixed in. There was a goat tee type beard, and thick horn-rimmed glasses, that must have been made from the bottom of two Coke bottles. The look on his face was more like he was confused; it didn't seem like he was angry with us. No, not angry at all.

"And who might you be," he looked Jimmy right in the eye.

"I... ah..." Jimmy answered. That was the best he could come up with.

"I don't believe you!"

"But..."

I was playing it smart, just staying out of it, and keeping my trap shut.

"And where pray tell did you come from," the old guy in the white coat could sure talk good.

"I...ah," Jimmy seemed to be stuck in that mode. So, he just pointed up, pointing to the top of the hill and to the sky.

"Another lie," the man accused Jimmy, " I was just up there, and you were nowhere in sight."

"But," Jimmy tried to spill it out again.

Just figured that the old guy was still out of it from getting bopped on the head with the Special Counterintelligence Mobile Unit. The old guy gave Jimmy another hard look, and that made him even more nervous.

"No honest mister, I came from up there," and once more he pointed to the top of the hill.

The man still looked a little bit like he didn't swallow that story, then he straightened the two Coke bottle glasses in front of his eyes and asked, "and what mode of transportation did you use to obtain flight?"

"No mode Mister."

Jimmy took a quick look around to see if he could find what was left of the briefcase. Since he was still getting unstuck, and trying to pull himself up, I showed him where it had landed, and got it to him.

"Thanks Shawn," he said, then he took the messed-up case, and handed it to the messed-up man. The guy looked at both of us like we were crazy. We were looking the same way back at him, so I guess that was all right.

After a few minutes of inspecting it, the guy said: "A flying briefcase, I don't believe it."

"But..." Jimmy was having a heck of a time getting two words together, and the strange man wasn't making it easy. He just kept the questions coming.

"Do I look like I was born yesterday?"

"You sure look a lot older than that Mister," my first words were gonna be the dumbest all night. At least I hoped so.

"And who is your anthropoidal friend," he looked at me.

"What did he call me?" I knew it wasn't good just the way it sounded.

"It means good looking," Jimmy said. I could tell he was lying. Jimmy was always good at smoothing things over like that, which wasn't easy to do when you were such a bad liar. So I guessed, he didn't want to tell me then, so I figured to ask him later. Like two seconds after, the strange old man began to try and get up. Jimmy tried to help push him up, but couldn't do a good job, because he was still half stuck under the guys two kinda heavy legs. I ran over to give the man a hand up. It wasn't easy; the guy had a lot of weight to him.

"Thank you, my friend," he said. Now I was his friend, a second ago I was an Anthro...whatever. Jimmy was a lot easier getting up.

One more time the man examined the briefcase.

"How did you ever get this thing off of the ground?"

"Well I didn't really..." Jimmy started to say, "You see I'm an inventor."

"So am I," the man for the first time seemed very happy. "Come, come it's getting dark, you must show me how this device works. Can you come to my laboratory?"

"La... bor...a...tory," Jimmy's eyes lit up. It was getting pretty dark, but I could tell by the sound of his voice that his eyes were lighting up.

Of course, Jimmy agreed, and I was along for the ride. We both collected our broken-up briefcases, and skate parts; and the old Professor went off into the bushes looking for something of his own. When he came out, he was holding this strange looking contraption. It looked like a milk crate painted black. There was a big hole in the front covered with glass, and motorcycle handles on the sides. I offered to carry the thing for him, but he wanted to handle it himself. It really didn't look like it was too heavy. Actually, it seemed like it was almost holding itself in the air, as we followed the man back along the dirt trail to his laboratory.

When the light went on inside the large white room, this time, I could actually see Jimmy's eyes, and they were already lit up. All of the chemicals lining the wall, the gas burners, the glass test tubes that sat at the worktable, all of the these things were things that Jimmy dreamed about for so long, and had seen in a bunch of horror movies. For the longest time he could not talk. His mouth just hung wide opened as he was taking it all in.

"It's not much, but its home," the man said. He then explained that he was Professor Burkhardt, a chemical engineer and physicist. That didn't mean too much to me, but Jimmy was impressed. As he talked, the Professor continued to check out the briefcase. Jimmy told the Professor who he was, and that he was also a scientist, at which the Professor was also impressed.

"Yes, I seem to remember you're an inventor, right?"

19

Jimmy bobbed his head and smiled. I wasn't asked who I was, so Jimmy said, that I was Shawn Malloy, a boy student, who sometimes assisted in Jimmy's experiments.

"Oh," said the Professor, as he seemed to look through me. "You mean like a guinea pig?" At first there was something about this guy that just turned me off.

Finally, the Professor placed the briefcase down onto the table.

"Okay, how does it work?"

The Professor was very disappointed to find out that the briefcase didn't actually fly.

"When we crashed, I must have floated too close to the ground."

"But how..." Jimmy tried to get out.

"My fault actually, I'm terribly fearful of heights."

"But what..." Jimmy was having a problem with words all over again.

"Is this what..." I said as I moved toward the box.

"Att, att, att," the Professor waved his finger, also interrupting what I was saying. The Professor wasn't the politest man in the world. "I would appreciate you not touching that." Stopped me dead in my tracks. His voice sounded nervous, like he thought the box might be dangerous or something. "But what were you boys doing out in the woods," now he sounded like he wanted to sidetrack us, and talk about something other than the box.

"Well sir, Jimmy answered. "Our experiment was a secret. Dead Man's Hill was merely the testing ground to keep my invention secure and private."

"Ah," the Professor answered, "you too understand the importance of secrecy, that is good Jimmy."

"And what were you doing out there sir," Jimmy asked before I could.

"That also is a secret," the Professor said.

We weren't gonna find out how big a secret for a good long time, a couple of months maybe.

The Professor offered us some milk and cookies. I thought he was joking, but Jimmy was anxious to talk to him some more, so we sat with the Professor, and had the milk and cookies. The Professor didn't say much; he more or less listened to us. Actually, he was listening to Jimmy mostly. Professor Burkhardt was still eyeing me like I was some kinda lab rat or something. Jimmy was talking about science class and all that junk. I was kinda bored, but politely didn't yawn in both of their faces. We got out of there kinda late, almost ten. Made sure I hurried home, so I didn't catch too much noise from my parents about where I was, and how I wasn't responsible. They knew I wasn't responsible, so why'd they have to yell about it all the time.

Jimmy asked the Professor if it would be all right for him to come back and visit, and the Professor said that it would be okay. Jimmy was as happy as could be.

The next couple of months we ended hanging out at the Professor's place a lot. Jimmy went even when I didn't want to go. Don't get me wrong, the Professor turned out to be a real cool guy, but I didn't dig all the talk about test tubes, and star gas, stuff like that. Remember, I was the guinea pig, so I just got involved when the brains were done with the experimenting, but too chicken to try the experiment out on themselves. Anyway, I'd be there when they needed somebody to test stuff out on.

The Professor must a got Jimmy to thinking a lot more, 'cause he was coming up with a lot more gadgets. To the briefcase, he added a small homemade rocket, honest, I wouldn't lie to ya'. It was hidden inside, next to the skate wheels. During the first testing, it didn't make us go any faster, but it made a large cloud of smoke that followed us everywhere we went. Jimmy told me that what he had actually made was a smoke screen, and that he had really planned for that instead of a rocket propulsion system. If he was happy with that story, so was I. Anyway, the smoke screen was pretty neat, and he called it the Ultra Diversionary Unit Nine. I don't know why he called it nine. We hadn't had an Ultra Diversionary Unit Eight, or even a seven. Yeah, I guess nine was the first, and that's because it just sounded cool.

The next couple of months the weather started to get warmer. Summer had come on kinda fast, and we were done with school for the year.

On a night warm and breezy, we arrived at the lab. The Professor wasn't there, and that was kinda odd, because he was almost always in there cooking up something. We knocked, and waited around for a few minutes, and just when we were about to leave, we saw him coming. He was still wearing his white lab coat, but it looked dirty and torn, like he had been in an accident. His face was scratched, and his glasses were broken. Another thing, he was carrying that black box with the motorcycle handles again. Me and Jimmy, we ran to give him some help. He looked like he was having a little trouble walking. Jimmy grabbed hold of the Professor, who just slumped onto him. I went to take hold of the box, and this time he just let me have it. He looked too weak to do anything else anyway. Then the weirdest thing happened. When I went to grab the handles, it just seemed like it was going to float away with me. Took a good grip on it, and it stayed with me, but it kept acting like it had a mind of its own. Another funny thing, for something the size of a milk crate, it didn't seem to weigh more than an ounce, maybe not even that much. Felt like I was holding a feather that was just gliding on the wind. Didn't know what to make of it. Jimmy didn't notice, he was too busy helping the Professor, and pumping him for information.

"What happened Professor?"

"It's no good, it's no good," the Professor whined.

"What's a matter, what's no good?" One thing with Jimmy, he was super curious.

"It's too dangerous close to the ground. I've got to learn to control it, can't do that low to the ground. Got to get higher, stop bumping into things."

"You mean," Jimmy looked at the box.

"No, no, no," the Professor shook his head, "can't get you boys involved."

"Seems like we're already involved," I said.

It was then that the Professor looked over to me, as if noticing me for the first time.

"Oh no, are you here too?" He didn't sound too happy to see me. "You boys have got to forget all of this, forget the box, forget me!"

"Maybe we can help," Jimmy sounded real anxious.

"No," the Professor whined some more, "it's too dangerous, too dangerous."

"Danger's our business," Jimmy came right back. Then he looked at me, "Ain't it?"

I wasn't really sure what our business was, but I said, "Yeah, sure," just the same.

"Just help me into my laboratory, then you boys will have to leave."

The Professor stumbled once more, and would have fell if it weren't for Jimmy catching him. He seemed groggy, and stumbled a little on the way back, but besides that he was fine.

Once inside the lab, the Professor collapsed on the chair at his desk. While he took a lot of deep breaths, trying to clear his head, us guys just watched him. There was only one problem, putting the goofy box down. Tried to lay it on the work table, but it didn't seem like it wanted to stay there. When I finally got it down, and took my hands off of it, it just stopped moving as if it were resting. It was like taking my hands away turned the thing off.

The Professor pulled another pair of glasses out of the drawer, and in only a couple minutes, he was thinking straight again.

"I want to thank you boys..."

But now it was Jimmy, who was cutting the Professor off. Seeing that he was back to normal, well maybe not normal, Jimmy turned all of his attention onto the box. His eyes bugged out of his head, as he stared at it long and hard.

"What is this thing Professor," he said.

The question seemed to make the Professor all nervous again.

"That is none of your business, so thank you very much, and now you will have to be going."

"Is that what made you get hurt," Jimmy asked. Jimmy still looked amazed, and couldn't stop staring even while the Professor answered.

"It's really getting late and I think..."

"What are the handles for?"

"That is..." the Professor started to say.

They just kept going back and forth, with nobody actually getting a question in.

"It kinda floats," I had to get my two cents on the table.

"Now one minute..." The Professor was still trying to send us on our merry way.

"Can that thing really fly?" Jimmy tore his eyes away to look at the Professor, and then went right back to the box. It was like he was hypnotized by it, and couldn't take his eyes off of it, well not for long anyway.

"Why are you doing this to me?" the Professor demanded.

"Touch the handles, it's really neat," I told Jimmy.

"What?" he turned back to me.

"Go on, do it," I told him.

"I must insist..." came from across the room, but the words were too late. Maybe they weren't too late; maybe Jimmy just decided not to hear them. If Jimmy had any weakness, it was that he was curious; so curious in fact, that even if he had wanted to obey the Professor, there was still that little voice inside of his head, that wanted him to grab onto the handles. It was that little voice, that usually got him in trouble, and me along with him. As Jimmy reached for the handle closest to him, he placed his right hand on the left-sided handlebar. That was the first time I saw it. It looked like a green beam of light that flashed out of the glass that covered a hole in the front of the box. The green light hit the beaker at the end of the worktable, and made it fly into the air, and shatter against the ceiling. It was so fast that it scared me and Jimmy too.

We all were ducking the falling pieces of glass, as the Professor shouted at us. "Don't, you'll neutralize all of our gravity..."

The Professor had tried to cut his own sentence off this time, but it was too late. Jimmy had heard him. He turned smiling back to the Professor.

"That's a flying machine, ain't it?"

Slowly, the Professor got out of his chair. He didn't seem like he wanted to tell us, but now he knew he had to.

"No, no, no! Nothing so crude." He cleared his throat, and paced for a second. "It's a gravity neutralizer."

"What," I said.

"A flying machine," Jimmy said back to me.

"No." The Professor seemed annoyed. "Of course, one may levitate with the device, but it has other, more practical uses."

"For instance," Jimmy was getting ahead of the Professor.

"For instance, with this instrument, one may reduce or increase the gravity of a specific object, or a whole area of objects."

Jimmy moved real careful around the box, this time being sure not to touch it. The Professor was watching him and me real close now.

"When do you think you'll have it perfected," Jimmy asked.

"It is perfected," said the Professor, sounding almost insulted.

"But it just exploded when I touched it."

"Because you touched it wrong. The mechanism is controlled through thought transference when one makes contact with the handlebars."

"But..." That's all that Jimmy got out.

"Wait, let me explain." The Professor was on a roll now. He was like a little kid showing off a new toy. Jimmy sure wanted to know what the Professor had to say, so he shut his yap fast enough.

"The machine was right, you were wrong. The left hand must hold the left handle, and the right hand the right handle, otherwise you confuse the box."

Didn't know that you could confuse a machine, but I had seen it. Guess it just took someone like Jimmy to do it.

"Then it really works." Jimmy could hardly believe it.

"It is the work of my lifetime." The Professor seemed real proud of what he was saying. Then he went over, and put his arm on the box, like it was his kid, or something.

"But it made you crash," I said.

"No, no." He shook his head. "It's not that box, its me. You see..." Now he seemed ashamed. "I am afraid of heights. And when one is only four of five feet off of the ground, there are a lot more obstacles that one can bump into."

"How high can it go?" Jimmy asked, still real excited.

"I'll take it up for ya'." I jumped right in.

"That is out of the question." The Professor answered me first loud and quick.

"How high can it go?" Jimmy asked again.

Again, the Professor turned, and put his arm around the box, this time it was like he was holding a baby.

"There is no limit, your imagination is the only limit. You see it neutralizes gravity, so that one's weight is no longer of importance. You could drift forever, or until you got too cold, or your oxygen ran out."

"Can you go anywhere but up?" Jimmy wanted to know everything.

"To be sure," said the Professor, "the box can also repel, or attract the gravity of other objects, buildings, trees, the Earth itself."

While the Professor was still holding onto his baby, Jimmy started to walk around the machine, taking it all in.

"But there's no dials, no switches, buttons, or anything like that." Jimmy kept looking. "How do you control it?"

"That's the best part," said the Professor. "Your mind does it all. The only limit my invention has, is that of the user's imagination. Think fast, the machine goes fast, think high, and it will carry you beyond the clouds. My problem is that I can only think four feet off of the ground."

"Let me take it up for a test run," I tried again.

"No, no, no." He sounded serious about it.

"But why?"

"Because, tell him why," he turned to Jimmy, who just shrugged his shoulders. "Because you know too much already, that's why, and you must promise me that you will tell no one."

"Secrecy's our business," Jimmy told him.

The Professor just shook his head, not sure what our real business was at this point.

"That's still not a good reason," I said to the Professor.

"You want a reason? I'll give you a reason." That's all he said, then he walked over to the chalkboard, picked up a piece of chalk, and screeched this out, d-1/2 at 23000-1/2 (32 ft. /second.) .2187. S=t213.7. sec-t. After he was done, he just stood aside, and looked back at me.

"So, what's that all mean to me," 'cause I really didn't know.

Then he looked at Jimmy, who walked over to check out the board. Then Jimmy looked over to me.

"It's the formula for terminal velocity," Jimmy said.

"Huh?"

"That's how fast you'll fall if anything happened to that box."

It was now that the Professor let loose with a loud clearing of his throat. We both paid attention. "Nothing will happen to the box," he pointed at the blackboard, "this is what will happen, if you should lose contact with the box." He seemed quite proud at having pointed that out.

"But I won't leave go," I told him. I wasn't that stupid.

"No," the Professor stood his ground, and was starting to sound more like my Dad every second.

"How else are ya' gonna test it?" I asked him.

"Yeah," Jimmy was right on my side.

"This is not a toy," The Professor explained.

"But you gotta test it out." Jimmy kept pushing for a ride on that thing.

"Yeah," I followed right behind, "and if you're too chicken, why don't ya' let somebody with some guts take it up for you?"

"And crash to the earth at a hundred and twenty miles per hour." The Professor was not happy about me hinting that he might be a gutless coward. Neither was Jimmy, who yelled at me.

"Shawn!"

"Sorry," I said.

"No, he's quite right, you know," admitted the Professor, "I am a chicken, but I cannot let you boys risk your lives."

"But risking our lives, that's our business," Jimmy told him.

"You boys have so many businesses, how is a man to keep track?"

Even I was confused about what business we were in at the moment, so before the Professor could say anything else, I told Jimmy to, "Shut up, will ya!" He seemed to understand, 'cause he shut up.

"Remember, I'm trusting you boys to keep this all a secret." The Professor then tried to drop the whole subject, like we had never even heard or seen his incredible flying machine.

"Now let me get you two some milk and cookies." He started to walk towards the door that connected the lab to the rest of the house. No way were we letting him off the hook that easy.

"Aw, come on Professor." I followed right behind.

"No, no, no!"

"How else are you gonna know how good it works?" Jimmy joined right in. We had stayed quiet about the subject for about as long as the both of us could. I'd say a good ten seconds, which might have been our record for staying quiet about anything. The Professor turned back to us, and looked down. I had a feeling, a good feeling he was gonna weaken.

"Would you promise not to go too high?

"Yeah!" I exploded.

"Go for it!" Jimmy jumped in the air like a little kid. We then grabbed each other, and began to jump up and down around the room. We were shouting and cheering, and for a minute we almost forgot about the Professor being there with us. Then I remembered, and let go of Jimmy. The Professor was shaking his head again.

"But not flying high, ain't that your problem," I said.

"Yeah." Jimmy reminded him too.

"Well but you..." the Professor seemed like he had lost his words someplace. "You... you must promise, you will not do anything stupid." He took a hard look at Jimmy. "I know, I know, being stupid is your business, but you must both promise me, secrecy, no horseplay, those two things I must insist on." Both me and Jimmy, we just nodded our heads. "Good, then tomorrow, I will start instructing you on how to use the gravity machine."

Me and Jimmy had another outburst of cheering and grabbing each other. When I caught a glimpse of the Professor, he was shaking his head again, and looking like he might have made the wrong decision. We calmed down pretty fast though.

I wanted to be good, extra good. I didn't want to look stupid, or act like a little kid, because the next day I wanted to learn how to fly.

CHAPTER 4. THE MISSION

We got to the Professor's place real early that next day. He wasn't ready for us that early, 'cause he was still having his morning tea. He invited us in anyway, and offered us some crumb cake that he had left over from breakfast. I wasn't hungry, and neither was Jimmy. We hadn't had any breakfast either, but who could eat. Didn't even sleep that night before. Well, I did force down a little bowl of cereal to make Mom happy.

While we sat around the kitchen table, inside of the old house, we watched the Professor finish off his tea. While he sipped on that, he talked.

"You must not ever think you are going to crash," he said, and pointed his finger at the both of us.

"Why not?" I wondered.

"Because," he took another quick gulp... "Are you sure you don't want any of that crumb cake?"

"No sir," Jimmy said.

"Same here," I told him.

"Its quite good you know," he kept trying to push those buns on us. We both just twisted our heads back and forth this time.

"Why can't we think about crashing?" I asked again, because the last thing we wanted to hear about were some old crumb buns getting staler by the minute.

"That is a very good question," he answered, picking up one of the buns, splitting it with a knife, and spreading butter on top. The big problem with the Professor was that he couldn't eat while he talked, or talk while he ate, and he was making us both very nervous. It seemed like it was taking him forever to spread a little butter on that bun. In between munches, he began to get the story out.

"If," he took another bite. He was beginning to drive me nuts. "Should you think of crashing, the machine will interpret that as what you want to do and…" More chomps on the cake, more grinding his teeth.

"And," I said, dying to know, and I wasn't sure I could wait for him to finish chewing.

"Oh, that is simple, you will crash."

"So, we should just think happy thoughts?" Jimmy smiled.

"We have to be very, very serious from this point on," the Professor said very sternly.

Didn't feel too happy about the crashing part, but if wanting to fly was something you wanted bad enough, you had to take the chance of falling from the sky. Both me and Jimmy looked at each other. I could tell that he wasn't happy either.

"At first," the Professor went on, "I was afraid to let you boys test my machine but..."

Then he stopped again to pick up some of the sugary chunks off of the tablecloth, and put them in his mouth. Do you believe this, I thought, and of course I didn't. This was going to be the most exciting day of my life, and we were putting it on hold 'til the Professor could clear the sugar off of that bun. I just hoped that we didn't have to wait for him to brush his teeth after.

"When I thought about it," he continued finally, "what could possibly go wrong?" He shrugged his shoulder, and washed down the dessert with the rest of the tea.

"Of course," he said, looking down at the other half of the bun, "I wonder if we have any marmalade?" Then he shook his head, "No," he said, "Got to watch the diet," and then he patted himself on the belly, and got up out of the chair.

"What could go wrong?" Jimmy was really curious about that question. He almost snapped. I guessed the Professor, and the never-ending bun had gotten on his nerves too.

"Oh, yes, yes... can't think proper on an empty stomach, you know?"

I just clenched my teeth, and forced a smile back at him.

"If you should happen to think about flying too fast, the air friction could set you on fire." That didn't sit too well with me either. "But that's ridiculous of course," he said right after. That I was glad to hear. "You will have gone unconscious, let go, and plummeted to the earth long before you could have reached that speed," and I was unhappy all over, that quick.

"The box can travel that fast?" Jimmy asked almost as if he didn't believe what he had heard.

"It is just as I have told you," said the Professor, "the speed, the machine itself is limited only by this," and then he took his finger, and pointed it at his head.

The rest of the day we were taught how to grip the handles that were stuck onto the box, and how we should make pictures in our head to make the machine go up, and other stuff. Other stuff was making the light shoot out of the front of the box, a green light, that made things rise up in the air, or make them so heavy that no one, or nothing could lift them up. The Professor showed us by raising the telephone on the desk just above our heads, and then putting it down, so that me and Jimmy couldn't lift it up, even with the both of us trying at the same time. Then he let us do it too. It was the neatest thing I had ever done, a lot like school, but only a good time.

The lab was too small to practice the actual flying, and since no one was supposed to see us, we had to come back when it was getting dark. We didn't know how late we'd be getting back, so with school being out for the summer, we had to find a plan to keep us out late that night. It was me that came up with the plan. Jimmy wasn't the only one with smarts. The old pup tent in my cellar hadn't been used in years, but our parents use to let us sleep in it, even though it was only in the living room. Maybe since we were older they'd let us move it out into the yard? That's what I was hoping for anyway.

It worked. Our parents were gonna let us camp out, if we promised not to stay up talking all night. We promised, and then set up the tent. That made only one problem to overcome; my Mom and Dad were usually up 'til around eleven. We didn't plan on meeting the Professor that late. Jimmy said, we should call up the Professor, and tell him we were coming later. That was all right by him, the later the better. Less chance of us being seen.

My folks were really getting on my nerves, it was already about eleven, and they were still making a lot of noise in the house. I knew the time, 'cause I could hear the news just coming on. Jimmy told me to just stay still and relax, but I was too jumpy for that. About eleven-fifteen staying still paid off, my Dad yelled out the door.

"Everything alright with you guys?"

"Yeah Dad, it's cool" I called back.

"Good night then, and don't stay up much longer."

"We won't Dad!"

"Goodnight Mr. Malloy." Jimmy yelled.

"Night Jim," and then my Dad closed the door, but he left the back porch light on lighting the place up like a football stadium.

"We'd better get going," Jimmy said.

"We'd better wait," I told him.

"But..."

"If my Dad looks out the window before he gets in bed, we're sunk."

"Darn, why'd he have to leave that light on for?"

"Probably for our safety."

"I hate that!"

"Just a couple a minutes," I told him. Now I was the one staying still, but I knew what he was feeling, 'cause he wasn't the only one dying to play Superman. We sat there, and just looked at each other with the flashlight shining in the middle of the tent. Waited about another minute or two, but it seemed like fifty. When I couldn't take it anymore: "Let's get goin'."

"Do you think it's okay? "Jimmy whispered.

"Hope so, I want to fly."

He smiled at me, and then flicked off the flashlight. In the dark his voice sounded louder, and I was afraid someone was gonna hear it.

"We're gonna have to run for it now."

"Shhh," I told him.

"We'll sneak out the back," he had lowered his voice, "move slow at first, and then bust a gut when it's clear."

That's just what we did. We crawled out of the tent. That stupid light was shining on everything in the yard. The idea of walking slow only lasted about two seconds, and then we both burst into a full blast sprint. As we jumped over the white picket fence, we heard the scary sound of my Dad's voice calling from the house. A second later, we stopped, and ducked down behind some ash cans in our neighbor's yard.

"Should we go back?" Jimmy asked me.

That was a hard question, because I was already in trouble.

"You two boys come back here this instant," I'm sure Dad was waking up the whole neighborhood. A couple of lights from other houses went on. Some dogs started barking.

"What do you want to do," Jimmy said again. He was as scared as me.

"If I go back, I won't be out of the house for a long time, tonight, I'm flyin'!"

"Let's go for it!"

Then we got up, and started running again. My Dad was still calling, the dogs were still barking, but we kept running just the same.

CHAPTER 5. UP, UP AND AWAY

The Professor was pacing up and down the linoleum floor of the lab when we finally got there. Think he paced a lot, sometimes on account of his nerves, but mostly I think on account of us.

"Where have you boys been?"

Before we could explain the Professor stopped us. "Do you see the time? I have to sleep once in a while, do I not?"

Guess he was right to be upset, but I had just risked never being allowed to watch television, or let out of the house again, so I was a little upset myself.

"Well we're gonna get..." that's all I got out, because Jimmy broke in with what was really important. Besides the Professor knowing that my parents were probably out looking for us, would've gotten him even more nervous.

"Time to get started Professor. Where's the box?" Jimmy asked.

"Humph," the Professor grunted, and then walked across the floor to a large wooden door that opened into a closet. Before he opened it, he stopped, looked at his watch, then at us.

"I wanted to keep this a secret, but twelve twenty is kind of a drastic security measure, is it not?"

We didn't answer, we just wanted to grab onto that box, and start soaring into the sky. He went into the closet, and came out holding the Gravity Box. Like always before it just seemed to be floating there. I mean he was touching it, but it was almost like he didn't have to.

"Okay, who's first?" he asked.

"Me, I'll..." me and Jimmy both said it at the same time.

"Well since Jimmy, he is the scientist..." and as he was speaking, I was starting to get mad already, because I knew that meant that Jimmy was gonna get the first ride. "...It is only fair that that he be the one to test the machine first."

I had always thought that the guinea pig did the dirty work first, and so what was fair about any of that?

"But..." I said, and they both looked at me, and I knew I was gonna lose that argument, so I just shut my trap.

As the Professor handed the machine to Jimmy, he looked like a kid with a new toy. Come to think of it, he was a kid with a new toy, the greatest toy in the universe. And I could tell from the look on his face that he wasn't worried about our parents being mad or nothing. Whatever happened tonight was gonna be worth all the punishment that we were in for when we got back home. Ten years worth maybe? I hoped it'd be worth it anyway.

Slowly Jimmy walked the machine through the door, and to the outside. The wind was blowing easy, and there were a million stars in the sky. For the longest time he just stood there holding the handlebars like he was scared to move. I knew the feeling, 'cause I was feeling it myself, but not as bad as him, it wasn't my turn yet. The Professor just watched, but didn't say a word. It took a little while, but then Jimmy got his nerve up. He coughed like he was clearing his throat, and then he talked.

"What now Professor?"

The Professor said two words that made it all sound so easy.

"Think up, just like we practiced!"

"That's it," Jimmy turned to him.

"That's it," the Professor shrugged his shoulders like it couldn't be any simpler. Jimmy's hands tightened around the rubber handle grips. I could see his whole body straighten up, like he was frozen or something, but he wasn't frozen, he was just scared. Then he closed his eyes, and we all waited, but nothing was happening. So, Jimmy opened his eyes, and looked at the Professor.

"See it boy, see it in your mind, relax and see it!"

Jimmy closed his eyes again. It must have taken a few seconds to see the picture, 'cause at first nothing happened. Then all of the sudden Jimmy let go with a gasp, he opened his eyes again, and his legs began to rise up in the air.

"What'll I do?" he seemed really scared now.

"See yourself going higher, not too fast," the Professor told him, and then he turned to me, as Jimmy started to move upward. "I did explain to you, that whatever is in contact with the machine will also have its gravity neutralized, if that is the picture inside of the brain?"

I wasn't too sure what that meant, but I couldn't answer anyway, my eyes were glued on Jimmy, who was now floating just over my head.

"What now?" he screamed, as if he were a hundred feet in the air. Jimmy was wanting more instructions now.

"Just think yourself a little to the left," the Professor told him.

Jimmy must have done just that, 'cause he started floating that way.

"Good boy, good boy!"

Now Jimmy was wavering back and forth. He had a stupid grin on his face, and I could tell he was really happy about being up there. Still scared, but happy at the same time.

"Okay, come on down," said the Professor.

"Thought you wanted to see how it maneuvered, need a lot of space, need to go higher for that," Jimmy called down like he was still far away.

"You're not afraid?" the Professor asked, as if he were amazed that Jimmy wasn't terrified, and seemed to be doing everything just right.

"Just a little," Jimmy told him, "but I want to do more, I want to go higher." His voice was shaking like he was a lot scared, and you could tell he was trying to get hold of his breath, that seemed to be running away from him. I could feel his excitement, and I wasn't even up there yet.

"Alright then, take yourself up a little higher, just a little."

"Let me have a turn," I was jumping the gun a little, but it looked so cool him being up there, like he was on the greatest amusement ride in the world, and I guess that was about as cool as you could get.

"Cut me a break, will ya,'" Jimmy shouted just overhead.

"When's my turn?" I asked the Professor.

He just looked at me long and hard, scratched his head, and said, "Stay here for a moment," and then to Jimmy, "You won't go away, will you?"

"You got it Professor," he answered, and Jimmy's head shook back and forth. Then the Professor walked back into the lab. While he was gone I talked to Jimmy.

"How's it feel?"

"Great!" That's all he had to say.

"That's all," I wanted to hear more.

"Nothing else you can say about it?"

Great huh, I thought to myself, and while I was thinking about it, a cloud went by hiding the moon. It made me look up, and then I thought how neat, or cool, or great it would be to be up there right now.

"Can't you tell me anything else?" I begged Jimmy.

He was thinking now.

"Okay," he said, "my body, everything, it feels like its not there."

"Huh?"

"Like I'm here, but I'm not. I don't feel like anything, like I'm empty, like ah... ah balloon. That's it! Like one of those big, hot air balloons floating in the sky all day, 'cause they're lighter than air. That's another thing, I feel lighter than air."

"Ah man", now I was really jealous. I didn't know what air felt like, I only knew that's what I wanted to feel like.

A minute later the screen door screeched open to the lab, and out came the Professor. At first, I didn't recognize what he was carrying, because I had thought that there was only one. He was bringing out a second Gravity Box. I ran right over to him.

"Gee Professor, I didn't know you had two!"

"Ah yes, actually this was the first one. I had to tighten the handle, but it is alright now."

"Can I... I mean do you think..." he didn't have to read my mind to understand what I was getting at.

"Of course, you silly boy, what do you think I brought it out here for?"

"Thanks Professor," and I went to grab it out of his hands.

"Calm down, calm down! It has not been used in a very, very long time. As a result, it may not react to command as quickly as the later model. For that reason, go slowly; stay high, above the trees. Keep away from my house, I cannot afford to be repairing the roof."

I laughed, but he didn't, so I guessed he wasn't trying to be funny. The Professor never was one to be joking around. Then he handed the first Gravity Box over to me.

"Be especially careful coming down. Lower yourself five to ten feet at a time, no faster."

Once the box was in my hands, I was as scared as Jimmy. Something in me wanted to chicken out, but there was no way I was doing that. As I held it in my hands, my whole body began to tingle. Started to giggle, it was something I couldn't help.

"Come on up, it's great," Jimmy called from up above.

And I giggled some more, still a little bit scared. Yet I wanted to be up there with him. So, I tried to stop being scared.

"Be careful," the Professor ordered.

Then I closed my eyes, and tried to think up, but nothing was happening.

"Make images in your head, your mind's eye must see pictures," the Professor reminded me.

Holding my breath, I started to close my eyes again. But before I did, another cloud started to pass in front of the moon. All at once my legs lifted into the air, and the box and me were shooting up in to the sky, like we had been fired from a cannon. I was zooming over a big pine tree before I knew it, and that was the most scared that I have ever been in my life. The scream came out of me from nowhere. From below there were calls coming from the Professor and Jimmy. Couldn't make out what they were saying, just that they were yelling to me.

Seconds later I was way above the trees. Don't like to say it, but I was ready to cry. The scream was still coming out of me. Jimmy was wrong; you could feel your body, like my stomach, that felt like it was trying to climb up into my chest. The Professor was wrong too; the box had worked real quick, too quick for me. Everybody had been wrong that night, especially me, 'cause right then, I didn't want to be anywhere near that cloud, but it was coming at me and coming up fast.

Didn't want to, but I looked down anyway. Could see two specks down there that looked like Jimmy and the Professor. It didn't seem like they were making any sounds that made sense, just a lot of noise to me. Now that I remember, the reason for not crying, I was too afraid to think of it. How to get down? Don't leave go of the handles. Those were the thoughts going through my mind. And they were racing through my head like a thousand miles an hour.

Had never gone that fast in my whole life. Been on the Thunderbolt roller coaster and everything, nothing like this. The Thunderbolt was one of the fastest coasters in the world. That's what the amusement park people said anyway. It was the wind brushing against my face that let me know I was moving with that much speed, and a whole lot faster than any old roller coaster. Then all at once, even the trees looked small. Jimmy and the Professor, I couldn't see them anymore. There was only enough light coming from the moon so I could see some of the trees below. Above them everything seemed too bright. Below, it was starting to look like a giant pit with no bottom to it. It was a great big hole that this scared kid didn't want to fall into. Even the moon seemed like it was shooting right at me. Then I remembered, it was hard, but I had to put the moon out of my head. Thinking about it could land me there. The cloud, had to keep that picture in my head. Had to think cloud. As afraid as I was, had to close my eyes one more time.

"Try to see the cloud, try to see the cloud," I kept saying that to myself.

Kept zooming up. Seemed to be moving faster. How could I be moving any faster? And I began to think; this is what a bullet must feel like when it's shot out of a gun.

"Cloud, cloud, cloud," I kept saying, screaming in fact, but it wasn't working. "Cloud! Cloud! Cloud!" My voice almost broke, 'cause the shouting was at the top of my lungs, but the darn Gravity Box wouldn't listen. It kept heading straight to the moon. "NO!" I screamed again. Had to get those thoughts out of my head. Then like someone had stepped on the brakes, the box and me coasted to a stop.

Must have been inside of the cloud now, 'cause it seemed kinda misty. It was glowing inside with the moon shining through it.

So, there I was floating in midair, don't know how high I was. Didn't want to think about that. When my eyes opened, below was nothing, but the top of the trees again, and miles and miles of dark. For a minute I could feel my eyes begin to get wet, but I still didn't cry. Wanted to but didn't. My hands were gripping real tight to the handles, and maybe I was shaking. Know my teeth were chattering. Was trying to think of a way down. It was one roller coaster ride this boy didn't want to take. Couldn't think of the ground, had to think of the top of the trees, something like that. Like the Professor had said, one step at a time. The moon kept bouncing in my eyeballs. Had to get the moon out of my head. I didn't want to think of that. Wasn't ready for that trip again. "Get out of my head you STUPID MOON," I yelled as loud as I could. For like the longest time, there was the moon, the stars, and me, oh and yeah, that stupid cloud. Stars... Stars! No! Get rid of that thought. The flying machine seemed to have me bouncing up and down, as I trying to force any thoughts of going higher out of my head. Had to think down, had to think top of the trees. In my mind the pictures began to appear. It was only there a second, and I started too fall. It was too fast again. Another scream came out of me. Couldn't help myself. The Thunderbolt had seemed like a baby ride next to this crazy thing.

"Think slow, think slow," my voice said to me. Like it wasn't me at all, but someone inside my head handing out the orders. Someone smarter than me, who was telling old Shawn to get out of the way. The picture was there, playing in my head, and it was like

47

magic, the box almost came to a dead halt, and started to ease down real slow. When it got to the top of the trees the box stopped, and I was floating in mid-air once again.

"YES, YES, YES THANK YOU," I yelled out, yes I was thanking the Gravity Box, and I meant it.

A minute later I heard a voice calling to me. It was Jimmy. "You okay?" his voice seemed far away as he called from below.

In a minute it became easier to see him. And I could see what looked like a green glowing light coming up at me from below. That was the light coming out of the front of the box. And his voice sounded like a little mouse from a Saturday morning cartoon as he was calling through the night air.

"Hurry man," I was still a little shook. All right, so I was a lot shook. I had just been through a major shaking up.

"Here I come," Jimmy called out. As he moved up, he seemed to be getting bigger, and he was sounding a little more like Jimmy as he got closer.

From the ground the Professor was still calling; "Is everything alright?" I was barely able to make out his words as they bounced off the treetops.

You could tell he was nervous by his voice, but not as much as me. Of that much I was sure. All that was important to me was getting down and in one piece.

"Hurry up," I called to Jimmy again.

In a second he was floating right next to me. Don't know why he was doing it so good.

"You okay?" he asked again.

"Do I look okay?" don't know why, but I was mad for him asking. "Get me down, I'm scared," and you know it didn't bother me telling him that. Being scared is something that you didn't usually tell other guys about, but right there and then, I didn't really care who knew.

"So am I," he told me, "but ya' know," and he got real serious. "We have a scientific test to perform."

"Are you crazy?" that was me yelling again.

"Thought you wanted to be Superman?"

"Superman ain't gonna fall a couple thousand feet, and be smashed to bits if he leaves go of this stupid box!" And that fast I started to plummet down.

"Think happy thoughts," Jimmy yelled to me.

"Happy thoughts, happy thoughts, up, up, up," I cried out, and started to shoot up again.

"Remember," Jimmy shouted out, "the box is listening."

And I knew what he meant by that; that if the Gravity Box thought that I wanted to crash into the earth, it might just try and help me do it. So I just tried to think something else, anything else. My breathing, that was the first thing that popped into my head. Don't know why I decided on that, maybe it was that my lungs were pumping a mile a minute trying to keep up with my heart, so it was the easiest thought to grab onto.

"Is everything all right?" the Professor was still calling out from the ground.

"It's cool Professor Burkhardt," Jimmy called back.

"It ain't cool, 'cause I'm scared." and I couldn't believe I kept telling him about that.

"Come on..." Jimmy started.

"I want down! But not to fast, not to fast," I looked at the box.

"But ain't it neat, just floating up here like this?"

"It ain't cool feeling like your stomach is gonna shoot out your mouth any second."

"If you go down now, you may never get this chance again."

"Don't think I want it man!"

Jimmy stopped to think for a minute. He didn't look at me, so I knew he was up to something. Probably trying to dream up away to keep me up there.

"Come on, let's go down," I told him. "If we were gonna discuss it, we were gonna do it on the ground."

When he looked at me he said: "Look, we're pals aren't we, best friends?"

"Best friends don't go trying to get best friends killed!"

"Aw, come on, just for a little while we can fly around."

"No!"

"You can follow, just keep an eye on me..."

"No!"

"It's all safe, all you..."

"No," I shouted, I wasn't gonna let him get any of his argument out.

"Alright," he said, "you win! Guess it's up to me now. Don't worry; you're my best friend. I won't tell anybody you chickened out."

When he said that, I knew right away what he was doing. I'd never been chicken, and Jimmy knew it. Not 'til now anyway.

"You're a real creep, you know that!"

He smiled, 'cause he knew what I meant.

"Then you're comin'?"

"We'll go real slow?"

"Hey, I'm scared too!"

"Can't we go lower?"

"That's when we'll run into trouble. Up here, there's nothing to bump into."

"I'm scared, I'm real scared Jimmy," said that hoping he'd let me off of the hook.

"But you'll do it anyway, right," but Jimmy wasn't letting me off of the hook.

My head just bobbed up and down a couple of times, 'cause I didn't want to say it. Wouldn't have believed it myself, that I had agreed to go along with him.

"Then let's do it!" Jimmy started to drift a little to the left. All I did was watch, and somehow my box knew that was where I wanted to be too. I began to follow.

"We should go up a little bit higher, just to be on the safe side," he called back to me.

"Don't tell me what's happening. I feel better not knowing." Next thing I know, we were gliding up and over that cloud that had caused all the trouble to begin with. Wanted to say something, but there was nothing I could say. After about a five, or maybe ten minutes it wasn't so bad anymore. It still made me nervous being so high and all, but it was kinda neat. I'm sure Superman must have felt something just like this, only this Superman was keeping a really tight grip on the handlebars.

CHAPTER 6. HIDE AND SEEK IN THE SKY

Ten minutes later we were soaring over the houses at the edge of the woods. Well not exactly soaring. Jimmy had kept his promise, and we were still traveling kinda slow. Funny thing, I wasn't really scared anymore. Must have been getting use to it. Being up in the sky I mean. Jimmy circled, and headed back into the forest. We had been back and forth across the wooded area twice. To be honest with you, I was starting to get bored. When I get bored, that's when I get dangerous. Because up 'til then I didn't have to do anything better to do. My gravity machine just seemed to follow his like a well-trained dog. It was like you didn't even have to think about any of it, it just happened.

"Yo Jimmy, why don't you let me handle the maneuvers for a while."He turned around kinda surprised; because that was the first time I'd talked to him since we started riding these things across the sky.

"Be my guest," he called back. He seemed kinda happy about it. The moon seemed to be shinning brighter since the clouds had drifted away. But I knew better than to pay any attention to it. Anyway, it was a lot easier to see what we were doing. We were still pretty high up, but the lights from some of the houses and streetlamps at the edge of the town made it easy to tell where we were.

"I'm going down for a look see," I told Jimmy, and then I started to go lower.

"But we're not supposed to be seen!"

Hearing him didn't make me stop. All at once it felt neat to be gliding down. The picture in my mind saw me diving slowly down then climbing back up again.

"Shawn," he called, thinking I had gone too far. That's when the picture in my mind made me fly up again. "Come on, don't fool around, this is a top-secret mission."

"That's no reason we can't have a little fun."

"I thought you were scared?"

What Jimmy said was true, I was scared, but not like before. Riding the box had started to remind me of the Thunderbolt. It was just scary enough to be fun now. Now I decided to climb higher, higher than ever before. This time it was going to be above the clouds.

"Where are you going?" Jimmy's voice trailed from behind.

The picture of being just above the cloud was in my head. It was like a movie, and in the movie, I was going fast, but not too fast. I knew I could think fast, but not too fast, or I would burn up on re-entry or something.

"Shawn," he called again, but that didn't stop me.

"Come on," I called back to him.

Right above the cloud Jimmy caught up with me.

"What the heck are you doing?"

"We're gonna test how well the Gravity Box maneuvers, right?"

"It's cold up here," he said.

"Right," I asked again, not listening to his complaint. "Scientific testing requires, that we see how well these levitation devices handle, in all situations." I was talking in his own language, so it would be harder for him to say no.

"Sure but..." Jimmy was trying to get out of it, but when you threw that science talk around, it was hard for him to refuse you.

"Let's do some dive bombs, and right before we hit the ground, we pull ourselves out of it."

"Are you crazy?" Where had I heard that before? I had stopped talking science too soon, and moved on to the crazy stuff too fast. Jimmy was back to just thinking that I was out of my mind. And that always made it harder for him to see my side of things.

"Come close, a couple hundred feet maybe..."

"Look Shawn..."

"You're not chicken, are ya'?" It was time to move back to the basics. If science and crazy talk didn't work, you could always just call him chicken.

"No, but..."

"Because if you are, nobody's gonna hear it from me!"

He just looked at me for a second. Jimmy knew exactly where I was headed with the old "chicken" talk. It was a great tool to use on a kid. It had worked already once tonight, only not on him.

"No. I'm not chicken. It's just that I think we ought a' make sure we can work these machines right, that's all."

"You're right," I said, "it is cold up here", and without saying another word I started my Kamikaze type dive to the houses below.

"Where are you... nuts," Jimmy was chasing right after.

The movie in my head was like this: The box and me are falling straight down to the ground. Fast, but not too fast, I start to drop.

We're about to crash through the rooftops. It would be a close shave, but not too close, if you get my drift. Then at the last second, we pull out of the dive, and put that rickety old Thunderbolt in the roller coaster graveyard.

Jimmy was right behind, still calling me names.

"You stupid..." The rest of the words I can't say. Strange thing is, that it was scary this time too, but I didn't mind. It was fun scary, like a monster movie, and somehow there was a difference. As I pulled out of the dive, and went soaring back towards the clouds, I just missed crashing into Jimmy.

"You stupid..." there were those words again. Think the only time he ever used that kinda language was on me.

Right after I passed him, I slowed to a stop, so that he could catch up. When he got close it became real clear what he was saying.

"This is supposed to be a scientific experiment, and you..."

Without giving him a chance to spill it all, I swerved in closer, and kicked him on the side of the leg.

"Tag, you're it!" Then in the movie in my head the Gravity Box was taking me fast across the woods.

"I ain't playing this stupid..." he called after me.

Maybe it was the night air, but whatever it was, it was making me kinda crazy. Jimmy would have said that it wasn't the night air, that I was crazy most of the time, but this was different, 'cause I was feeling extra crazy tonight, and right in my hands was the power to be as nuts as I wanted to be. I mean who could have stopped me. Not my parents, not the police, not even the army. Sure, they could send up a missile or two. Then I'd just have to outrun them, or shoot a beam at it to make it too heavy to fly. 'Cause all I had to do was to think I was faster, and I was, or picture that missile dropping out of the sky, and it would. The Professor had said it, the Gravity Box was limited only by my imagination, and I had plenty of that to go around. Hanging with Jimmy, playing spy all the time, you needed to pretend a lot, so I had that on my side. There was a whole bunch of pictures in my head that could let me go anywhere, and do just about anything.

"Stop playing around you..." Jimmy was catching up quickly. He must have seen himself moving faster than me.

He sounded pretty mad, so I stopped, and floated over Dead Man's Hill, which I could make out below because of the lights shinning out of the paint factory that was nearby.

"I've had it with you Shawn," he shouted as he glided along side of me. "We're supposed to be conducting a scientific experiment, not acting like a couple of kids. We're doing this for the Professor, to let him see how well his invention works, how it maneuvers."

As usual, Jimmy was using good judgment. My Dad didn't think I had any of that. But from being around Jimmy, I learned that good judgment could always ruin a good time.

"Maneuvers pretty good," I said, trying not to get him any madder.

"Yeah," he answered, not really wanting to agree with me. "There is one other thing."

"Yeah," I said, waiting for the ax to fall, "what's that?"

"You're it!" He said it so fast that he caught me off guard.

Then he gave me a quick kick in my leg, and he was off and running, or should I say flying.

"You creep!" Had to laugh though, 'cause it was funny. Could hear him laughing too as I set out after him. Jimmy was moving real swift now, climbing higher and higher, and then dipping down real fast just as I was about to nab him. He was still laughing at me, and laughed some more every time he'd dodge me.

"You're gonna pay for this pal," I couldn't stop laughing myself. Never in my life had I had this much fun. We were soaring over trees, and in and out of clouds. All at once Jimmy changed the game into one of hide and seek. He slipped inside one of the large gray clouds, and just stayed quiet and still. Had to move in real slow to try and track him down. There wasn't a sound, except for the wind blowing by.

"Know you're in there pal," I said as I slowly drifted into the next cloud. Funny with all the racing around, the cold didn't seem to be bothering me then.

"Come on out you coward, and play like a man," I was trying to get him to laugh again, but nothing happened. The next cloud was the same, just a lot of empty space. Gliding upwards, then looking down still didn't help. Then it came to me, an idea to flush him out.

"You know what I'm gonna do, don't ya'" I yelled out, "I'm gonna make a picture in my head of all the clouds getting super heavy, and falling down, then you'll be easy to find."

"Nooo!" Jimmy screamed, and flew out from the cloud he was hiding in. He came right to my side. "You goofball," he sounded upset, "you shoot a beam like that at these clouds with me inside, and I'd get squashed on the ground too."

"Yeah, I thought about that."

"And you were still gonna do it?"

"No, I just wanted to tell ya' one thing."

"What?"

"You're it," I kicked him back, and was off and flying again. Within seconds we were back in town. Jimmy was closing in on me real quick now, so I tried one his tricks, climbing so high, and then taking a nosedive. My box had gone lower than I probably should've, but the houses were pretty easy to see.

"Not so low!" He shouted from behind.

But it was so cool flying over my friends' houses. I wanted so badly for them to know I was out there, and what I was doing. Then I went a little too low, 'cause there was one of those big circular antennas sticking up, and I didn't see it. The box cut right on through it like it wasn't even there. A piece of metal clanged on the cement, and I was moving up again.

"See what you did?" Jimmy was still after me.

About thirty of forty stories up, I stopped and waited for him.

"See," he yelled at me, "told ya' to stay up high!"

"It was an accident!"

"That's always you're excuse." He wasn't buying it.

"Whoever it belongs to will find the piece tomorrow, and put it back on his roof."

"Its not totaled?"

Didn't answer him, he was right, so it wasn't a good time for me to argue. When the other guy's right is never a good time to argue.

"Let's test the gravity neutralizing beam, then we'd better head back."

"Already," who wanted to go back? Going back meant giving the machine up, and going home to Mom and Dad, who were very unhappy with me at the moment. What they had in store for me, I really didn't want to think about. That much I was sure of. I mean eventually I would have to pay for the crime, but for now, I just wanted to hang out in the clouds, and put that punishment off for as long as possible.

"The test will only take a few minutes, and besides the Professor's probably getting worried."

"Aw man!"

"You know I'm right."

"You're always right, at least that's what you always think."

"Let's not argue right now, we've got a job to do."

"How come you're always the boss?"

"Shawn…" Jimmy said, sounding like he really didn't want to argue.

Down below a light went on in the house without the antenna.

"Come on," Jimmy said, spotting the glow coming out of the window. This time I was with him as we scooted across the town. Now we were staying high, and out of sight.

When we got over the area of town where all of the stores were, we stopped, and just floated again. It was pretty well lit, because of all the neon signs, and stuff that the different stores used for advertising. That's when I saw it, the perfect test for the neutralizing beam.

Old man Jenkins was the guy who ran the only supermarket at that end of town. He was a mean old guy, and he had kicked me out of the store one time, when I had asked for a job as a box boy. What a creep he was. I found myself getting some nasty thoughts when I saw his big delivery truck parked down there under a tall streetlamp.

"Got it," I told Jimmy.

"What." he said.

"The way to test the beam."

"How's that?" he asked.

"Down there," I nodded my head at the truck.

"Can't do!"

"Why not?"

"Too big. If the beam isn't strong enough, we could get it so high, and then wreck that thing."

"Come on, it'll be a blast. We take old man Jenkins' truck, and put it on his roof or something."

"No," he said still sounding like he was the boss again. "Suppose it crashes through?"

"Well then, let's just move it across town, or something like that."

"Too heavy."

"I'm doin' it!"

"No!"

"Who died and left you boss!"

"The Professor said..."

61

"He didn't say anything about you being the boss."

"Let's find something else, work our way up to the truck."

I could tell what he was doing. He was trying the old psychology on me again. Trying to get my mind off of Jenkins' truck for a while, then we'd never do it, but that trick wasn't working this time.

"I'm putting that truck," I told him, "over on Maine Street."

"Don't do it, Shawn."

"Stop me!"

"But what if..."

"Limited only by the pictures in my head, ain't that what the Professor said? Now who's being unscientific?" It was the only thing that I could think of, I was throwing the Professor's words right back in his face, and enjoying it very much.

"He said something like that," came back sounding like he really didn't want to agree with me.

"Well, I can see that truck a hundred feet in the air over Main Street."

"But somebody's liable to see," Jimmy was the only one arguing now.

"I'm doin' it," I told him again. And then I closed my eyes.

"Shawn... Shawn..."

Jimmy kept trying to change my plan, but all I wanted to do was to see that big old truck up there in the sky with me.

"Get off my back," was keeping my eyes closed tight, while I saw in my head that monster of a truck rising up.

"Shawn," he kept trying to stop me, but I couldn't wait to see the look on old man Jenkins' face in the morning.

All at once the truck was starting to leave the ground, in my mind at least. When my eyes opened to check it out, the green beam glowed, and shot out from the front of the box, and hit the truck.

There was another loud "Shawn," from Jimmy, and then he kept quiet, as the front end of the truck began to rise upwards in my head.

Closed my eyes a second time. Jimmy was being real quiet now. I guess he figured if I got distracted, that that old pile of junk would crash through the street. Behind my eyelids the whole truck was leaving the ground. When I opened my eyes, the real truck was rising up too.

"This is great," I shouted, because I was too excited to keep my big yap shut.

"Hope you know what you're doing," he finally spoke. I knew to expect that from Jimmy. In my head the truck was right up in the sky with us. All at once the beam shot out brighter. So bright in fact, that I almost couldn't look at it. Jimmy had to close his eyes when the truck popped into the air like it had been sitting on a powder keg. It blasted up, and was headed straight at us.

"Shawn," Jimmy screamed.

We both dodged the giant truck just in time as it whizzed on by us. All at once being so scared, my mind was no longer thinking about the box, or controlling the gravity of the truck. The bright green ray had thrown the delivery truck up over our heads about a hundred feet, and then switched its gravity back on. All at once the truck

63

started to fall to the street below, like a meteor falling to earth. Both me and Jimmy flew out of the way. The truck was still falling. I didn't know what to do. It looked like it was going to land right onto old man Jenkins' store roof after all, but not the way I had planned it in my head.

"#$%*&", Jimmy cursed and loud. Never heard Jimmy use words like that.s

Would have swore something myself, but my mouth just wasn't working right then. It was falling fast, too fast, and it was gonna crash right through the roof of the old building. Closed my eyes again. This time, 'cause I just didn't want to see it. My grip on the handlebars got tighter, and I could feel my whole body grow tighter too. Then out of nowhere, there was a crackling noise. That made me look one more time. Another blinding flash of green light had blasted out of Jimmy's gravity machine, and shot like a lightening bolt across the sky striking the truck. The big panel truck halted in mid-air, and bobbed up and down, like it was floating in a giant pool.

"Jimmy," I tried to say, but he wasn't interested in hearing me now, he was concentrating real hard on the action below, real, real hard.

Then easy like, he glided the truck just over the top of the building, and had it floating above the pavement. Jimmy was handling the Gravity Box like a pro, but I guess when you were dealing with knuckleheads like Shawn Malloy, you had to be a quick learner.

"Thanks Jim..." I said, but he looked at me real fast and hard, so I knew not to bother him, not yet. He still had to keep his mind on what he was doing. The green beam took the truck out over the street. Slowly he was putting it back down. It was only ten, eleven feet from the ground, when a set of car lights came turning around the corner. Being at the opposite end of the block, our view had been cut off by one of the taller buildings. What turned the corner was a police car.

"Oh no!" Jimmy cried out.

The car screeched to a halt, only a short distance from where the truck was about to land.

"Let's get out of here!" That was my idea.

"Not yet," Jimmy was still trying to put the truck down safely.

Only three or four feet from the ground, two policemen jumped out of their car. I'm betting they couldn't believe what they were seeing. I'm sure that it was the blinding light of the bright green beam, and us up in the darkened sky that kept them from making us out.

"Come on," I said, and I meant it.

"Wait," Jimmy said, and the beam all at once died out. The truck dropped to the street. The two policemen jumped back, afraid that the truck was gonna topple over on them. We heard the crash as the truck bounced off of the asphalt. A tire exploded, and one of the cops screamed like a little girl when the truck landed close by to where he had been standing. I guess no one had ever thrown a truck at this guy before. Then me and Jimmy got out of there as fast as we could. All that was in my mind was that the police were gonna try and shoot us down. But we were like human bullets ourselves speeding across the sky. Guess they didn't shoot at us. At least we didn't hear anything. They were probably more scared than us. Who wouldn't be, seeing a truck being lifted up in the air by a strange green beam? Probably thought we were some alien creatures from Mars, or Venus, or who knows what they were thinking. Only knew what Jimmy was thinking, and it wasn't nice thoughts as we stopped over an empty clearing inside the forest.

"That was the dumbest thing you've ever done."

"Well, it worked out alright didn't it," and I had just followed up the dumbest thing I had ever done, with the dumbest thing I had ever said.

"You could've done a lot of damage back there."

"I'm sorry," I really was.

"You're always sorry, and I'm sick of hearing it!"

"Just don't hang with me then. You won't have to listen to me anymore!" Didn't really mean that, but I had to say something. Let him know I didn't care if I ever saw him again, which was a lie, a big lie. Just had to let him know it anyway, even if it was a lie. From there on in it usually turned into a shouting match to see who could yell the loudest, and being a couple hundred feet in the air wasn't changing our usual routine one bit.

We shouted back and forth for a while. There were some mean things said, yet nothing bothered me too much, until Jimmy said, "You're no longer involved with this experiment, when I tell the Professor what happened, you won't be allowed near the lab."

"Why don't you just go and tell 'em, you big baby!"

What he had said had made me real mad. First of all, he sounded like he was my Dad giving me orders, and more important, we had never ratted on each other, not about anything; and believe it, between Jimmy's crazy experiments, and my stupid stuff, we had plenty of dirt on each other.

"This is too big, too important for you to be playing dangerous games with."

"Aw get off my case, do you're dumb experiment by yourself!" Then I saw myself moving away from there, and that's when it happened.

"Hey, come back, where you going?"

"Don't know, and it ain't none of your business."

"If you take that, it's stealing!"

"It ain't stealing, this is what's known as a joyride." As I started to move further away, he called me again.

"Shawn! Don't!"

"You ain't my father," and then the box and me zoomed away.

Jimmy was right after me, but then I played his trick back on him. I made the box pull into another cloud.

Jimmy kept calling, "Shawn... Shawn!" The cloud was good cover. Couldn't see him, but he couldn't see me neither. The box stopped dead in space.

Didn't want to move too fast anyway, in case Jimmy moved into the cloud, and we'd crash.

"Shawn," his voice sounded like it was getting further away.

Slowly the picture in my head was of me coming out of the cloud for a look around. The box and me began to rise up slow like, and it stopped right where I'd wanted to.

Far across the night sky was a distant green speck moving along, and about to disappear, that had to be Jimmy. I ducked back down again into the cloud.

Waited, waited for what seemed to be a real long time. After awhile there was this rumbling noise. Couldn't figure out what it was. Wasn't the other box, 'cause that didn't make any noise.

When I peeked out of the cloud again, the whole sky had turned gray, and hard to see through. It was like a giant fog had rolled in. The moon was still there, but now even that looked dull, and further away.

"Shawn," came another call. Jimmy was real far away now, and I could just about make his voice out. Couldn't see him at all, yet the harder it was to hear Jimmy, the louder that rumbling sound got. After turning around a couple of times, I still couldn't see anything. Just could hear the rumbling getting louder... louder... It felt like the whole sky was shaking in fact. It was like any second a giant dragon was gonna come tearing through the darkness of the night. Yet it wasn't a dragon, or even the other box with Jimmy coming after me. The thick cloud had hidden it for too long. Suddenly, red and white lights came pushing their way through the night sky. A giant plane was not far away, and moving fast, and headed right at me.

For a minute I thought it was gonna crash right into me. Somehow seeing the plane in my head triggered the box, and had me flying directly at that plane at lightning speed. The dumb box and me started whizzing across space, straight into the flashing lights.

Couldn't help screaming at the top of my lungs, again. Playing chicken with a jet plane can do that to you. Was doing a lot of screaming that night, and I think I was ready to lose my voice from it all. Waking up with a sore throat was the least of my problems. I was just about to have a head on collision with a giant passenger plane. Only about twenty, thirty feet from the jet, I figured out what was happening. Had to get another picture into my head, and fast.

The moon was the only thing that could be seen with the jets blinding lights right on top of me. I grabbed hold of that picture, of that vision in my head. With only a second before crash time with the plane, the box rocketed upwards, shooting me into space. The wing of the giant airliner had just missed me.

Climbing higher and faster than I have ever moved this time, I was ready to cry all over. I didn't feel like stopping the tears, not this time, but first the Gravity Box had to be stopped. Began thinking, thinking real hard. Wanted to be down there, back on earth, wanted to hear my Dad yelling at me for running away. Even wanted to admit to Jimmy that what I did was wrong, and dumb, and what a goofball I had been all night. Maybe I'd get grounded. Get told I'd never be able to leave the house again. That was all right too, 'cause there was no place I wanted to be more than home, and safe right then. Wanted all these things, but the box wasn't listening. The crazy machine was still climbing to the moon.

"I'm sorry," I yelled at the Gravity Box, but it wouldn't listen.

Thinking something I had done had broken the machine, and it would only move upwards. Maybe thinking about the moon so hard, had stuck the machine in some kinda moon mode, so that it couldn't change directions now. Something I had done had broken the Gravity Box, and it wouldn't listen to me anymore. The rest you know. I'm back in the Professor's lab, waking up on the table, and wondering how I got there. And I was serious about what I had said: I was ready to go home, get yelled at, and get my punishment. But I wasn't about to get that lucky. After almost doing a head on collision with an airliner, and landing on the moon; and just when you thought you couldn't top the bad things that had happened that night, things were just about to get worse, and a whole lot more dangerous.

PART II. THE BAD GUYS IN BLACK

CHAPTER 1. WHAT HAPPENED WHEN WE GOT BACK HOME

The guys in the crazy hoods dressed all in black, were just the icing on the cake that night. When we were sure they were nowhere around, we had started back home, to face the music there.

"What do you think they wanted," I asked Jimmy.

"Probably spying on the Professor. They want the Gravity Box I bet."

"But how'd they know..." then a terrible thought, "You don't think on account of me... That was so stupid!"

"No, no, can't be. They're here too soon. They wouldn't have been able to track us down this fast. If someone had reported an Unidentified Flying Boy, they might send someone to check it out, but they would probably just think it was a crazy phone call."

I was feeling so bad. "You know I tried to get the box to listen to me, but it wouldn't. After the plane almost hit me, that was it. Tried to come back, tell ya' how sorry..."

"It wasn't your fault, a wire came loose or something. You had the old machine remember?"

"The Professor said it'd be fixed tomorrow, no problem."

"How mad was he?"

"He wasn't happy, but we can't worry about that now. We gotta find out what those guys are spying around for. Remember, counter espionage, that's our business," he said, and he was serious.

"What about the police, maybe..."

"It's a secret project, no one can find out, remember? Besides who would believe us?"

"I'm sure those two cops we almost dropped the truck on would buy into our story."

"It's top secret, nobody can find out..." Jimmy said again yelling at me this time.

"Somebody already found out, and we ain't real spies, we're just kids, what are we gonna do?"

"The Professor's our pal, right? If he's in trouble, we gotta help him, don't we?"

"But how?"

"Didn't figure that one out yet. First, we gotta come up with a good story for our parents, why we took off in the middle of the night."

The idea of that made me think that fighting spies might not be all that bad.

We were still trying to decide on a good story, when my house came into sight. Some of the lights were still on.

"We're almost there," I said. "Think, think!"

"Why don't you come up with something?"

"You're supposed to be the genius."

"Geez, it must be after three, maybe four."

"We're sunk and..."

"Shhh," Jimmy warned me, as he grabbed onto my arm.

That was the second time he had done that to me that night, and the second time I liked it even less. When I stopped to look at what he had stopped me for, I saw two men running along the side of my house. They were the same men who had been hanging around Professor Burkhardt's place. At least they looked like the same men. All dressed in black, hiding in the shadows, gliding along the wall.

"Holy..."

"Shhh," Jimmy said again, "Get down!"

Jimmy dropped to his stomach, and I was right behind. He started crawling, dragging himself with his arms. Besides being spies, we were trained commandos; at least when we got tired of being spies. Tonight, the two jobs seemed to go hand in hand. We were into a lot of different businesses. Jimmy was anyway.

We were quiet as could be as we slid along the grass into my yard. Lying on the ground behind a big hedge, we could see everything. The first guy to reach the house ducked under the window, just like it had happened back at the Professor's place. A second guy stopped on the other side of the window. The light was still on in the living room. It was probably my Dad waiting up for me. So, while they were looking in, we were watching them. They were kinda sneaky about it, standing back a little in the dark, so nobody inside could see them out there. We were hid right behind the big hedge doing the same thing. If I hadn't been so scared, all this might have been exciting. But almost crashing into the moon was enough excitement for one night, so the spies in my backyard, I could have done without.

The yard was still lit up from the porch light, but then suddenly went out. I jumped, and almost cried out again.

"Why would my parents turn out…" I started to say.

Jimmy "shhhh" me right away.

Me and Jimmy being back far were pretty much out of it, but we could still see each other a little.

"Do ya' think…"

Jimmy put his finger to his lips, and pointed to the roof. Across the ledge of the second floor was a third man moving along it. Didn't see him before. It was like he had come out of nowhere. There was still another guy that hadn't showed yet. Where was he? Could be anywhere, since none of them were still making any sound.

"What do you think they want," I whispered in my lowest voice.

"Don't know, maybe you."

"Huh!" Got a little louder that time, maybe too loud. Jimmy reached over, and put his hand over my mouth, which was something I should've thought of myself. He twisted his head to the bushes near the street, which meant that he wanted me to go there with him. We crawled all the way over to that spot. It was far enough away from the house that we would not be seen, and we could speak a little louder.

"Let's get to the back of Johnson's house," he said.

"But…"

"Let's go," he ordered. Darn, I hated when he did that, but I was sure he had an idea. I know I didn't.

Across the darkened street we sprinted on our toes, so we wouldn't make much noise. When we got there, we hid around back.

Mister Johnson had a garage that was separated from the rest of the house, so we could talk pretty easy back there.

"What about my Mom, and Dad, and my little sister," I was having trouble catching my breath.

"They're safe, I think!"

"How can you say that?"

"Because, I think they're waiting for you."

"I wish you'd stop sayin' that!"

"Well we saw those guys at the Professor's place, and you're the only link in your house to the Professor."

"Aw nuts... why didn't they go to your house?"

"Maybe they did..." he thought for a minute, "but I don't think so."

"Why not, why me?"

"Because, whoever they are, they know a little about us. Probably know we camped out at your house tonight. Probably figured we'd come back here."

"Maybe we should get the police," I said again.

"Maybe your right," he surprised me. Jimmy didn't let me be right much of the time.

"Let's check on them one more time, if the coast is clear, we'll split on over to the station house."

Real easy like, we both popped our heads around the corner to that old run-down garage. For a moment we didn't see anything.

"Maybe they left," I said, "put one of those bugs on the house and left."

"Maybe," Jimmy spied a little more. "If we call the police now, they'll think we're a couple of crazy kids."

"Not if we can show them that bug thing. Do ya' think..."

"Shhh," he stopped me in my tracks again, and every time he did that it, meant Jimmy had spotted more trouble.

This time I looked harder too. On this night of being nearly scared to death a hundred times, I saw scariest sight I had ever seen. From across the way, into the window that was the living room, one of those dark dressed men pushed my Father back. They were in the house now. Saw the guy in black holding something in his hand that might have been a gun. We were too far away to be able to tell, but it scared me real bad.

"My Dad..." Jimmy had to stop me once more by throwing his hand over my mouth, and pulling me back.

"Keep it down, keep it down!" His voice was still real low, but I could tell he wanted to scream it out.

"Now we gotta get the police," for a second, maybe third time that night I was crying.

"That's exactly what we can't do now."

"But my Mom, and Dad, my little...!"

"They're gonna be safe, at least 'til you show up..."

"But why?"

"Bring the police in now, and who knows what they might do. Whoever they are, they're trained professionals. One thing trained professionals don't want are witnesses."

"Don't say that," that really upset me, and made my stomach feel sick. "Then what are we gonna do?"

"We're gonna sit, sit, and think."

"Maybe we should go back to the Professor's."

"They'll know, the minute we show up there, they'll know, I have a sneakin' feelin' that's where mystery man number four is. Either with the Professor, or waiting around for us to come back there."

Everything Jimmy said I liked less and less.

"We gotta think this thing out."

"But we ain't real spies," I told him again, "we're just kids, that's all!"

Right then Jimmy turned to me, and gave me the most serious look he'd ever given me in his life.

"In there," he looked over at my house, "we can't do anything. Out here we can move, out here's where we got our chance."

Didn't know how much of a chance it was we would have. Inside my house were secret agents, real secret agents, or Ninjas, or whatever, and we were just a couple of scared kids. Even in the dark behind that old garage, I could feel Jimmy's eyes looking right through me, and I knew that if anything was gonna save my parents tonight, it was gonna take that big, old brain of Jimmy's to do it.

CHAPTER 2. THE PLAN

I was keeping a close eye on my house for what seemed a pretty long time, while Jimmy sat on the ground thinking this thing out. Couldn't see much. The light in the living room was still on, and I thought I saw my Dad move in front of it once. The guy in black was right behind him though. We were pretty far away, so I wasn't sure, just hoping that was Dad, and that he, and my Mom, and my little sister were all right.

"Think of anything yet," I said looking down at Jimmy. He could tell how upset I was.

He started to shake his head, like no he didn't, and then before he could do it, he changed his mind. He stopped, and looked up at me. There was an idea there, could see it in his face when he stood up to tell me.

"Ya' got something," I got all excited.

"Keep it down, we ain't that far away."

"Okay, okay," I whispered, "what ya' got?"

"First we sneak on over to my house. We get the briefcase, and load up on some gadgets I cooked up for just such an occasion."

"You really thought something like this was gonna happen?"

"You never know," he looked at me hard, and then I knew that he had always been ready for something just like this. "If the coast is clear over there, we head on over to the Professor's."

"What good's that gonna do?"

"If we can get hold of the Gravity Boxes, we can use them to rescue your parent's."

"How's that?"

"Easy, we bounce those creeps off of the ceiling."

"Cool," that sounded good to me, and I was game. At least it was better than anything that I could come up with.

"Come on," Jimmy said, and we started out through Mister Johnson's yard. We were gonna run, but first we had to walk, softly, 'til we were further away from my house. As we tiptoed over the flowerbed, which we didn't notice 'til we had trampled a couple hundred dollars worth of tulips, a terrible thought came to my mind.

"Got a bad idea in my head."

"Try not to think bad, we gotta think we can do this, or we can't!"

"But I gotta tell ya'."

"What's wrong?"

"Nothing, but what if... what if that other guy's waitin' over at your house, or even worst, what if he's at the Professor's lab like you said. If..." and it was a really mean if, "if we can't get to the Gravity Boxes, we can't help my parents?"

"Hmmm," that's when Jimmy went into some more deep thinking then, "Come on," he said, and started walking again.

"Do ya' got it," I asked him.

"Sure!"

"Well, what are we gonna do?"

"Easy, we're gonna cross that bridge when we come to it."

"Good plan," I said as I rushed to keep up with him. Soon as we thought it might be safe, we began running.

"Slow down, slow down," Jimmy told me. "We gotta run all way over to my place, and then back out to the Professor's. At this speed we'll never make it."

"Can't we take your bike?"

"Good idea, if the garage isn't locked. Gonna be tough enough moving around my house without getting caught. Breaking into the garage will really be rough."

"Then why don't we just head out to the Professor's?"

"I told you dummy, he might not be alone out there. The Professor might have company, that other guy, or maybe, they have more guys working with them."

"We're cooked," I said.

"Whatever's going on, we gotta have some way of dealing with them."

"You sure you know what you're doin'?"

"Have I let you down yet?"

Didn't answer him as we kept on jogging along. Right then Jimmy was my only chance to help my parents and my little sister, so I didn't want to get him mad at me, or make him lose his confidence. That seemed to be the real fuel that Jimmy rode on. After a second, when I didn't answer him, he just told me to "shut up", and kept on moving.

It was still dark out, so it wasn't as late as we thought. The streets were really strange now, dead like. No people, no cars, no nothing, except every once in awhile a dog would bark when we passed. No time to worry about that, so we just kept moving. Didn't get too far when a pair of headlights came at us from the opposite direction. Because the streets were so dark, the car lights seemed extra bright. At first, they blinded us.

"This way," Jimmy slapped my shoulder to get me to follow him. Quick like, we raced over, and hid behind an old junker parked next to the sidewalk. Both of us squatted, and leaned against the side of the car.

"Do ya' think they saw us," I said.

"Don't know," Jimmy kept his voice real low.

"Who do ya' think it is?"

"Don't know that either, could be nothing. Right now, we can't take any chances."

The headlights now lit up the whole street as the car came closer. We could see the lights glowing across the top of the car we had ducked behind. The sound of the motor grew louder. They were right on top of us now. Then the worst thing that could've happened happened. It stopped. As the car halted, the engine seemed to work even harder just sitting there. Me and Jimmy just looked at each other and held our breaths. We knew not to say anything. Then the car door opened. We heard their voices. It sounded like there were two of them.

"Did you see something?"

"Looks like somebody ran over that way."

By the sound of them, they might have been police, but even the police were something we wanted to avoid right then.

"Whatever, they took off in that direction."

"Want to have a look around?"

Then for the longest time the other one didn't answer. Me and Jimmy just sat scared, and waited for somebody to say something. Mostly we just wanted them to go away. Then the footsteps of one of those guys came moving our way. My chest tightened up, and it felt like I couldn't breathe. Felt like I was gonna die. Tap, tap, tap, his shoes clopped onto the street. He only took a couple of steps, but now he was practically on top of us, standing on the other side of the car.

"They could be right in one of those yards, watching us," we heard one of the men say.

Right after there was a clicking noise, and a beam of flashlight shot over our heads, and shinned into the yard in front of us. Could just about hold back the gasping sound in my throat. Jimmy must have heard me, 'cause his head twisted real quick to look. It was pretty dark, but in the shadows I could see the scared look on his face. The flashlight waved back and forth a couple of times, and then clicked off. The footsteps now moved away, going back to the car.

"Probably long gone by now, " the other man said.

"Probably."

The doors slammed shut, and after a second the car took off. When I started to get up, Jimmy grabbed me, and pulled me back down.

"Hold on for a minute," he said.

"But I wanna see..."

"So do they!"

"Don't you wanna to know if they were police, or those other..."

"They weren't the police!"

That threw me, 'cause how would he know. Jimmy could see as well as I could, and I couldn't see anything.

"How do ya' know?"

"Something I noticed."

"You saw something?"

"No."

"You heard something?"

"No."

"Well what then?"

"We were only a couple a feet from that car when they opened the doors."

"So?"

"Police radios' have a constant read out of everything going on. I didn't hear anything."

"You're scaring the heck out of me!"

"I'm scaring the heck out of me! We're gonna have to be extra careful now, they know we're onto them."

"Just what I needed, more good news. How'd ya' figure that out?"

"By now they know we're not at the Professor's. If we were going home, they know we would've been there by now. Most likely anyway, that's why they got people out lookin' for us."

"So what now?"

"We still go to my house, only now it's gonna be a little harder."

"You don't think they got your parent's do ya'?"

"Gee, I hope not... I kinda think not."

"Why not them?"

"Because, it won't do them any good, not yet. See they had to get to your parents, 'cause that's where we were headed; or maybe they thought we were already there. That's it! They thought we were already there, or they would've tried to capture us before we got to the house. Anyway, they'll want to get as few people involved as possible."

"But your house..."

"Oh, they'll be watching it alright."

"Then there's no way!"

For a long time, Jimmy didn't say anything, so I figured he had agreed with me. I was starting to feel real sad, thinking all hope was lost. Finally, he came out of his thoughts, and spoke to me.

"Oh there's a way alright. We're just gonna have to play at their game."

"Huh?"

"Gotta plan!"

Was glad to hear it, just wanted to know what it was, and if it was likely to work as the first plan.

"Well what is it?"

"Come on quick!"

"Where we going?"

"Take off your shirt."

"Why?"

"Because, its bright white, too easy to see."

Sounded like a good idea, he still didn't tell me what was up. I took off my tee shirt.

"Can you tell me now..."

"There's a gas station on the way to my house."

"So what?

"If they're gonna be hard to see, we're gonna be hard to see."

"How are we…"

"Invisible!"

"Huh?"

"We're gonna beat them at their own game. We're gonna become invisible."

After tonight, I guess anything was possible. For a while I was Superman, and now I was going to be the Invisible Man.

CHAPTER 3. HOW WE BECAME THE INVISIBLE MEN

Jimmy was right about the gas station. Only it wasn't exactly on the way to his house. Really, it was five blocks out of our way, which is probably why I didn't remember it. Since I was in a kinda daze, I wasn't paying much attention to what he was saying anyway. Kept thinking about my Mom, my Dad, my little sister, and how maybe all this stuff that was happening was my fault. Jimmy said it wasn't, but how could he be sure?

The gas station was all dark, except for the office that was lit with bright fluorescent lights. Guess that was to keep the crooks away. The place was dirty and greasy, so what did Jimmy want with it? Tried to ask him, but he just shushed me up again, and pulled on my arm like I was dog on a leash or something. He dragged me to the side of the garage, so if anybody came by they couldn't spot us.

"You'd better come back to earth man," Jimmy said, then he shook me by the shoulders, 'cause he could tell my head was someplace else. It took me a minute, but I got back to him.

"Huh, ah, Jimmy I'm so worried about my Mom and Dad and…"

"So am I, but walking around with your head screwed on backwards ain't gonna help anything."

"Okay, you're right, what do ya' want me to do?"

"Don't ask a lot of questions," which I did sometimes instead of just listening.

"Just tell me what to do."

"Camouflage!"

"Camouflage?"

"Well grease," he said.

"That wouldn't have been my first choice. Go ahead," I told him.

"Since we can't get to any dark clothes right now, we've gotta make ourselves dark, as dark as they are, as dark as the night." He was sounding real mysterious. Sometimes Jimmy did that too.

"Grease?"

"Grease!"

"But all of the grease is inside. We can't break in to get it."

"Maybe we don't have to. Most service stations keep steel drums around for the old stuff they take out of cars, and sell it back to the oil companies. They clean it up and all... Well anyway this place has a drum in the back I'm sure. When I brought my bike in to get air, I saw it."

"But you said grease!"

"Grease, oil, what's the difference, it's all black!"

"Would of thought of oil, before grease," I said to myself.

"What," he heard me just the same.

"Nothin'. Hey, why did I have to throw away my shirt, if we're gonna be covered in this stuff?"

Jimmy thought hard for a minute, "That's a good question."

"Well," I said.

"Your shirt was bright I ah…" He stopped for a minute, and thought, "Didn't think of that okay, but after we save your parents, I'm sure they'll buy you a new one."

Just shook my head. It was true; I had bigger things to worry about then some dumb old shirt.

There were a couple of drums in back of the gas station. It was dark, so we had to move slow, and do a lot of guessing about where we were stepping. The top came off pretty easy on the first drum we tried. Jimmy stuck his hand in, and felt around. We lucked out. He pulled out a dripping hand of slimy stuff.

"Pay dirt," he said, "it's hard to see back here, can't tell if my hand's dark enough or not." Holding the hand up to the sky, it was still hard to see, so we figured it was the good stuff.

"Its old and dirty, so it'll stick! The new stuff wouldn't work as good."

We covered ourselves with the dirty, old oil, making sure not to get it in our eyes. It felt pretty scummy, but I was thinking that even new oil wouldn't have felt too much better. Our pants were dark, so we left them alone. I was really glad about that. The filthy, old oil really gave off with a stink. We smelled like a couple of old cars that had broke down on the highway, and left for junk. Both of us were wearing white sneaks, so they got the filth treatment too. Was half waiting for Jimmy to give the soaking ourselves in filthy motor oil a special code name. Something like, Special Anti-Surveillance Camouflage Solution Number Nine. Nine was always a good number, but someday we really had to move on to a Number 10 or something.

Yuck, it felt awful. What was worse, our sneakers squeaked when we walked, 'cause we had over done it, wetting them with the oil.

"They may not see us," I told Jimmy, "but they'll hear us comin' a mile away."

"Maybe not, maybe after a couple of blocks we can walk enough to squeeze the extra oil out of the soles."

I was just glad we weren't going to be walking over my Mom's rugs later that night.

"Better hurry, be light soon. Then we'll have to jump into a barrel of white paint or somethin'," I told him.

Jimmy didn't answer that; he just said we'd better check the clock in the office to see the time. The reflection coming out that window gave us the first look at ourselves. We were a mess, but we were as dark as the night, so I guessed we'd be hard to see. The clock said it was five minutes after nine. That was obviously the wrong time. So we stopped at a little tailor shop along the way that was also lit up, and had a wall clock. Four-twelve the clock read, earlier than we had thought if the clock was right. It felt like we had been out there so long, but maybe it just seemed that way, 'cause we were in big trouble.

"That gives us about an hour, maybe a little bit more before the sun comes up," said Jimmy. "At least we have some dark to play with."

"That still isn't much time, is it?"

"Right now, we don't know how much time will be enough," he said. "That's why we'd better hustle. We're gonna run, but we're not gonna go too fast. Gotta save our energy."

So, we moved on. Jimmy was the leader. We were taking all the back streets and alleys along the way. We were trying to be super quiet, but still there were a whole lot of dogs barking, and the loud squeaking of our sneakers was making that impossible. But Jimmy was right again. The sneakers weren't making much of that squishing sound at all as his house came into sight. We slowed down, and the rest of the way we were walking, walking real slow, 'cause we didn't know exactly what we were walking in to.

CHAPTER 4. THE RAID

Spent more time on my belly that night then ever before in my life. Crawled under the beat and rusty cyclone fence that was around the yard next to Jimmy's house, but still we couldn't be sure just how safe we were. They were more invisible than we were, more quiet anyway. So if the place was being watched, or if anyone was inside with his parents and his little sister, we really couldn't take the chance on them spotting us. We weren't doing any talking for a while, mostly just watching. The plan had been set before we got there, so we really didn't have to do a lot of talking.

All the lights were out, and Jimmy was hoping and praying that his parents were just asleep inside and alone. Maybe my parents hadn't called them about us running away, maybe that was the reason all of the lights were out. It was kinda late when we were caught running away, so my parent's might have held off on making that call. Whatever, I knew it was still in the back of Jimmy's head that someone might be in there with his family, someone dangerous. I'm sure he was holding onto the same fearful thoughts that I was.

We watched real long and hard, and didn't see anything. So we crawled over towards Jimmy's yard. The cyclone fence at that end of the yard was much tighter with the ground, so there was no way we were sliding under it. Had to climb over. A lot easier being seen going over the fence, but there wasn't much choice. I was up and over easy. Jimmy wasn't as good a climber as me, so it took him a little longer.

That dumb old fence clanged as he wobbled back and forth before jumping off, and landing right next to me. Could feel my insides churning as the rocking fence kept screeching, even after Jimmy was on the ground.

"Keep it down, will ya'," I almost yelled, but then he "shushed," me real fast. We crawled a little more, before we thought it was okay to get up on our feet.

Following Jimmy, we headed around to the back of his house. We lucked out, his dog was in the house, and that old hound wouldn't be much help anyway. The back porch was gonna be our way in. In the door was another smaller door that let in old Ricky. Ricky, that was the dog's name. The door was there, so that he could get in and out without bothering anyone else. It was kinda a tight squeeze, and Jimmy already told me that he couldn't make it through. Me being a little skinnier, he figured maybe I had a shot of getting through.

"Suppose the guys in black are in there," I whispered.

"Then we're sunk," he whispered back.

"Should I get the door for ya'?"

"No, it makes too much noise, we might wake up Ricky. Go to my room; get my briefcase, and the other stuff we talked about. Its in a box under my bed."

"What if it's too dark for me to see?"

"Along the walls of the hallway, there are a couple of night lights my parents put out for my little sister. When you get in my room, close the door easy, and turn on the light."

"What if I run into Ricky?"

"Don't..." that was a very good answer.

"But..."

"Let's just hope that don't happen. He sleeps in my parent's room so..."

Hoping was the main thing I was doing as I slipped through the small swinging door. Jimmy told me that he'd be over at the garage, trying to get the bike, and a couple other gadgets together.

It was a tight squeeze, and the wooden door scratched my back, which only had oil protecting it now. I clenched my teeth, so I wouldn't cry out. In a minute I was in the kitchen. Jimmy might have been right about the upstairs hallway, but the downstairs was pitch black. Since we both hanged out there a lot, I tried to remember where everything was, but it seemed so different in the dark. The white refrigerator was the easiest to make out, since some moonshine coming in through the window was bouncing off of it. My hand grabbed onto that, and that helped me get halfway across the kitchen. Since there was nothing around it, that first part was easy. Kept thinking how mad Jimmy's Mom was gonna be the next morning, when she saw the big grease slick across the fridge. Hoped that was all she had to be upset about.

The wall was next thing I touched. This place was gonna be a total mess the next day. In a second, I felt the light switch. Wanted to flick it on real bad, but Jimmy had warned me not to chance it before we got to the house. We didn't have much choice about the light in his room, if I was gonna get all his things together for this, the biggest mission of our lives. Making my way across the carpet in the dinning room was a little rougher. I was reaching out for a china closet that should have been close by, but somehow just wasn't where it was supposed to be. That room in the dark seemed all wrong. Nothing was where I thought it should be. Everything was either too close, or too far away, and nothing felt right. The closet with all the dishes shook something terrible, when out of nowhere it seemed to jump right out in front of me. That was it, didn't want to go any further. Then I remembered my parents and my little sister. Old Ricky still hadn't heard me, or smelled me, or whatever dogs do before they go into action. The steps, I climbed up on my hands and feet, taking it real careful, 'cause Jimmy's parents were kinda close by now. Kept hoping and hoping that they were the only ones up there.

The nightlights were on just like Jimmy had said they'd be. On the balls of my toes my feet took me to his room. There was a whole lot of creaking, but there was nothing to do about it. I wanted to be like those guys in black, who just didn't make any noise. Kept thinking that any second someone was gonna run into me on the way to the john, or good old Ricky would be hot on my trail, and it'd be game over.

Everyone seemed to be tucked in for the night. On the way a low rumbling noise made its way to my ears. It stopped me for a minute. Couldn't make out what it was, and it seemed to be growing louder as I got closer to Jimmy's room. It was the kinda noise a motorcycle might make if it was stopped at a red light. Only the driver was revving the motor, like he was trying to impress somebody with how loud he could make it get. Thought it might just be passing by the house or something, but it just seemed to be getting louder and louder as I moved down the hall. Soon I was outside of Jimmy's room. And the strange rumbling seemed to be shaking his room. I was

94

afraid that somebody was inside, but why would they have brought a motorcycle into Jimmy's room? We were too low for it to be another airliner. I took a deep breath, and got ready to enter.

The door opened easy enough, but let go with a screeching sound when it closed behind me, and I was sure that it was gonna be heard by everyone in the house. So while I stood not moving for what seemed to be a very long time, I waited for someone to come, and investigate. Yet nobody came, and still the terrible rumbling filled the air. I was scared out of my mind, but I had no choice but to move on.

Whatever horrors lied in that room I had to face if there was a chance of saving my Mom, Dad, and little sister. The light switch was easy to find too. It was right on the wall next to the door, where it had always been. When the lights went on it almost blinded me, because my eyes had gotten so use to the dark and the dim light of the hallway.

The first thing my eyes saw was giant handprint pasted onto the door, and a big black smudge next to the light switch. Couldn't even imagine what a mess the rest of the house was. Oh, there was one other thing, lying across Jimmy's bed was a big brown retriever named Ricky, snoring his brains out.

Lucky for me he was still sleeping, and he looked like he might sleep forever. In fact, it was the first time I'd ever heard a dog snore. Ricky had been the cause of all that noise that was filling the house.

That snoring was probably the reason that Jimmy's parents had made the old dog sleep in Jimmy's room. Any other time I'd a just laughed, but I was too scared to find anything funny right then. I

95

was still on my toes as I moved near Jimmy's desk where the briefcase was lying. Wasn't making much noise, and what noise there was, Ricky's snoring was covering up. Lifted the briefcase off of the desk, then came the tricky part, getting the box that was underneath the bed. Ricky's eyelids were rolling back and forth, and he started growling, but he was still asleep. Then he started breathing real heavy, think he was dreaming. Guess old Ricky was off in doggy land chasing squirrels up a tree or something. What else could dogs dream about?

The box was slightly larger than the bottom of the bed, so the cardboard rubbed, and screeched against the wooden frame. Lucky for me, Ricky was a heavy sleeper, and still chasing those squirrels.

His face was right near mine as I was edging the box out from underneath the bed. Ricky's breath was terrible, like someone had just fed him an onion sandwich or something. What made it worse, was that he was now growling kinda loud, like he was in the middle of a dogfight, or going three rounds with the neighborhood alley cat. What a nut. The box had only a couple of inches to go, when Ricky let go with a loud yelp and jumped. Maybe I should say, we both jumped. Then he opened one eye that was looking me right in my face. For a minute it seemed like he was trying to figure out who I was. You know how it is, when you first wake up in the morning; everything looks like a big blur. Well, I guess it's the same for dogs.

"Good boy," I said real low, trying to get him to remember me real fast, and to stay on his good side. Out or nowhere that crazy dog yelped again. Not like he was mad or anything, more like he was glad to see me. Why is it that dogs make as much noise when they're happy to see you, as when they're trying to rip ya' apart? My heart almost popped out through my chest.

"Good boy, good boy," that's what I said, while I started to pet him like I had never petted him before, but the crying, and carrying on only got worse as I began shushing my brains out.

"Please, please Ricky," I started begging now, but Ricky wasn't about to show me any mercy as he let go with still another loud howl. Never knew he liked me so much, might have been better if he hadn't. The neighbors must have heard all that yelping, and all I could think to do was to keep petting him, and trying to coax him into being quiet.

"Good boy Ricky," what else do you say to a crazy dog? "You're a good boy, but you're gonna get me killed."

Was waiting for Jimmy's Mom and Dad to come bursting into his room any second. Then as fast as Ricky started, he stopped barking, and began licking my face with that big sloppy tongue of his. He was licking off all of my camouflage. I was so glad to have him quiet, that I didn't care. While he was busy slapping me in the face with his big, sloppy tongue, I was busy taking the stuff out of the box Jimmy thought we'd need. It only took a minute to move around all the junk, and to find what he had wanted. Now I had to find a way to say goodbye to Ricky, so he wouldn't flip out on me again. Petted him once more, keeping my face just in licking range to keep that big mouth of his quiet, while I took Jimmy's schoolbooks, and supplies out of the briefcase, and laid them on the floor. Put the other junk in there, and closed it up. There was still no sign of Jimmy's parents. Must have figured what a screwball dog they had, and decided not to pay him any mind. At least I hoped that was the reason that no one had come barging in on me and Ricky. There were a few more licks when I rubbed him on the head.

"And Jimmy was worried about the noise that the back door was gonna make," I whispered to Ricky.

He was being a good dog now, so I eased myself to my feet. Asked him to be good, and walked over to the door. His eyes watched me real close. That made me worry that he was gonna start howling all over again.

"Please," I begged once more, and then he looked at me just like he knew what I was saying. Before I opened the door, he laid his head back onto the bed, but still watched me very closely, and panting heavy like. After I turned off the lights I couldn't tell what he was doing. Probably he was back asleep before I was out of the room. He was a kinda lazy dog when he wasn't being crazy. There was a little screeching when I opened the door, so I decided not to close it all the way on the way out.

Had to be extra careful going back down the hallway, everyone was probably wide-awake now, 'cause of the way Ricky had said hello to me when I got to Jimmy's room. On the toes, on the toes, my head kept telling my feet.

Getting to the steps was easy, 'cause it was easy to see. The stairs wasn't hard, 'cause of the banister that just guided me down. Then came the hard part. Everything looked black again. Wanted to be extra careful not to bang that briefcase into anything. The large wooden china closet was the first thing I thought of. It was getting kinda easier to make my way by the time I reached the dining table, 'cause my eyes were starting to make out things even though it was dark. The dark didn't look so dark anymore, and the kitchen was just in front of me.

My greasy hand was still feeling its way along the wall, but it was easier to take my steps, being able to make out the shapes of everything in the room. Then the kitchen table was just about a foot away. Grabbing onto that made me feel real good, 'cause the door was right on the other side of it. Started to slide my way around that, when a loud thumping sound came from the upstairs. That froze me right in my tracks. It only took a minute to figure out what had made that noise. After the thump, came a heavy clumping sound that seemed like it was moving right over my head. Ricky was up and moving. The noise raced along the hallway, and down the stairs. Now I'm thinking, I should of closed that darn door all the way. He was coming after me. That made me afraid that another wild yelping session was also headed my way. The whole house seemed like it was thundering now as that big old dog plopped down the steps.

Then I had a more scary thought. What if Ricky didn't know it was me in the dark? Half blind, half crazy, he might think I was a burglar or something. Clump, clump, clump, the sound came closer and closer.

"Ricky, Ricky," I called out quiet as I could, but just loud enough that he'd know it was me. I was trying to add to the noise he was making as little as possible. He stopped when he heard my voice. "Don't bark, don't bark, please" I was begging Ricky in a whisper. He waited, we both waited. Didn't want him to get spooked, so I called him again almost like in a whisper.

"Ricky, come on boy."

That was it. Once he knew it was me he got all crazy again. He started howling, and running right at me. Must have been able to see better than I thought, 'cause he jumped right at me, and landed with both paws right on my shoulders, and acting like he hadn't seen me in ten years.

That knocked me back against the table, and then the table bumped into the wall. Falling back, I landed on my butt, and Ricky was right on top of me licking away. I could hear the salt and peppershakers on the top of the table topple, and begin to roll. Knew I heard them or something moving across the table. It seemed to be coming closer... closer to the edge. And there must have been other glass or china stuff rolling around too, 'cause there was that terrifying sound of things about to be broken. You know that scary sound right before the crash that made your Mom come racing into the kitchen, to see who knocked one of her new dishes onto the floor. And the noise had been extra scary, 'cause it had given you just enough time to know what was gonna happen, but not enough time to save the stupid dish. And that's what being in Jimmy's kitchen was like, you knew something was gonna come crashing down on ya', but knowing didn't matter, 'cause in just seconds the glass and junk were gonna be shattering all over the place anyway.

Whatever had been on the top of the table seemed to be rolling forever on its way to the edge, and I was just waitin' for this rain of falling china, or whatever to come showering down on my head. So, I held my breath, and I waited. And strange as it seems, Ricky waited too. He had stopped with his vicious attack of licking and yelping to wait with me.

Even in the shadows of that dark kitchen, I could see his big head looking upward as closer... closer... something was getting ready to come crashing down. For the longest moment there was nothing, and then something hit the floor. Pretty sure that it didn't break, but it made an awful racket, and as quickly as he had stopped, that screwball dog was acting like he hadn't seen me in years all over again. That made me sure that someone must have heard from the upstairs. Had to get out of there.

"Get off a me... get off," then I tried to push Ricky off of me while he licked my face all over again, like it was an ice pop or something. Again, the only good thing about that was while Ricky was painting my face with his tongue, and slobbering all over me, he wasn't making as much noise.

Tried to put his paws down. They were cutting into my shoulders and chest. "Ow, ow, ow," I almost cried out loud. Ricky wasn't trying to hurt me, but just him liking you could be painful. On top of everything, Ricky had me bent back so far that there was no balance in my legs. Luckily, I had one arm free, so I could reach back, and push myself up onto my feet. Did this all without dropping the briefcase. Then Ricky dragged his feet down my body, and his paws took some more skin with them as he landed back on the floor. Wanted to cry out again, but we had made enough noise for one night. Still no one from upstairs seemed to notice. That seemed real strange to me, and for the first time I thought about it that way. Heard of some heavy sleepers, but these people were unreal. At least I hoped they were sleeping?

Ricky was no sooner done shredding the skin from my chest, when he went to his water bowl, and started slurping down some water. I guess being crazy was a lot of work, 'cause it made him real thirsty. And let me tell ya', that old dog couldn't even slurp down water without making a racket. Couldn't wait any longer, had to get back through the door, my skin was torn, and my face was soaked in dog spit. If Ricky gotten any friendlier, he could have possibly killed me. There was some light coming in from the porch window, and the door was right next to that. Slowly I felt my way down to Ricky's entrance, and pushed the briefcase through. I followed right after. It was a tight squeeze again, and once on the other side, I didn't like what I saw.

CHAPTER 5. WHEN IT LOOKED LIKE THE END OF THE ROAD

When I got through the small hatch at the bottom of the porch door there was Jimmy. That wasn't what was bothering me. It was the man dressed all in black standing next to him that I really didn't like. Like before his face was covered, so you couldn't see what he looked like. He was holding Jimmy by the arm, and Jimmy's bike was on its side next to them. My feet stopped dead in their tracks.

"He was waiting for me when I came out of the garage," Jimmy said really sorry, and scared like.

"Shut up," said the man. His voice didn't sound mad or anything, just like he was handing out orders, and kinda like he was use to doing it.

A second later a large black van pulled up outside of Jimmy's yard. We just looked at each other. It felt like our gooses were cooked.

"Sorry," Jimmy said again. But he really didn't have anything to be sorry about. He hadn't caused all of what was happening.

"Shut up, I said," the man warned us again. This time he sounded a little angry. Guess he wasn't use to being disobeyed. I was shaking too much not to listen to him. It was my guess that it was the missing number four guy standing in front of me. Now the door opened to the van, and another guy stepped out. From where we were, he looked like he was dressed the same as the others. He was coming our way, and all I could think to do was to stand there, and keep shaking. This time I was definitely too scared to cry.

"You two boys walk over to the van," said the man, his voice still low in telling us, and once again it was like there was no feeling in his words. Both me and Jimmy didn't move. "Now," he said, and that time he sounded angry again. We turned towards the van. The other man came closer.

"He let me get all the way back to the house, then he sneaked up on me," Jimmy said.

"Shut up," this time the man pushed Jimmy on the shoulder.

It was the sudden crashing sound against the door that made the man look away from us. As Ricky burst through the hatch, and it swung back, all of us were caught by surprise. His big, old butt seemed to get stuck for just a second as the crazy dog pulled himself through the door. The giant retriever was barking with joy as it leaped off of the porch steps. Ricky jumped right onto Jimmy's shoulder, and kept yelping. The whole neighborhood must have heard him now.

"Get that mutt..." the man started to say.

And I'll be honest with you, don't know where I got the nerve, but I took that briefcase, with all the junk inside, and smashed the guy closest to us right across the back with it. Guess I didn't want him to hurt Ricky. This made him trip, and fall side ways over the bike. Now the other guy in black started running at us, and that's when the other door opened on the van, and another man got out. How many of these guys were in there? Seemed like one of those clown cars in the circus with a bunch of guys packed in.

Ricky seeing the downed man now saw his chance to lick a brand new face. Knocked the guy down again as he was trying to get up. Next thing you know Ricky was on top of him wiping his face clean. What little face he could get to with the guy wearing the mask.

"Get this mutt..." this time he was yelling, not so nice, like before. Did I say nice? So much for being quiet and secretive.

"Give me that case," Jimmy screamed out.

The second guy was almost on top of us now. Jimmy grabbed the case from me. Just like a trained spy, quick like he flicked it open, and took out the rocket blaster. That made me think that Jimmy really had been planning for something like this for a long time. The second man was just getting close to us with his friend not far behind.

"Get the bike," Jimmy yelled at me again.

While Ricky was still making a fuss over the man on the ground, who was trying his darndest to get up, I pulled the bike from underneath his legs. As fast as he'd push Ricky away, that good old dog was back showing this guy just how much he liked him.

On the side of the rocket was the switch that was really a cigarette lighter that Jimmy had found in the trash. Jimmy flicked it once, but it didn't light. Back on the ground, the man had been able to push Ricky off of him just long enough to pull something metal and flashy out from his coat. Whatever was in his hand had caught the light for a second as it came out into the open. Ricky in no time was headed back at a third try at giving the guy a savage licking. All I could think to do was to block the dog with my foot.

"No Ricky," I called. Ricky was stopped only a second, and then tried getting around me to be with his new and dangerous friend.

105

The second flick of the lighter on the side of the rocket did the trick. The lit fuse zipped right up to the rocket, and set it off. It started shooting sparks like a bunch of Roman candles right at the guys charging in at us from the van.

Everyone seemed a little slowed down by this except me and Jimmy, 'cause we knew what was happening.

Old Ricky was not fazed by the shooting fireworks blasting by him. I took another shot at pulling Ricky back, but that dog had a terrible streak of friendliness that was not easy to turn off. Guess he thought the bad guy on the ground wanted to play, 'cause old Ricky was about to go after the guy in black again.

This time the man on the ground seemed ready with the metal device in his hand, ready to go off, or to come down, or whatever it was supposed to do. All this was a lot easier to make out now that Jimmy's: Anti Bad Guy Deterrent Device No. 9 was sparkling up the sky. Ricky was a pest, but I liked him, so that bike made a perfect battering ram to stop whatever evil the guy in black was aiming to do to Ricky. He yelled out when the wheel rammed into him. I guess he was hurt, or something. But none of this could stop Ricky, who was stopping that guys every attempt to get back on his feet.

"Get this %&^O* dog off of me," the guy screamed. Can't repeat exactly what he said.

Still that thing was in the spy's hand, and I could see it shining every time another flash of light shot out of the rocket blaster. Since the bike had worked to stop him before, this time I rammed his arm even harder. He yelled again when the wheel ran over his wrist. His hand opened up, and my foot kicked whatever was in his hand out onto the grass.

What was blasting out of the back of the rocket had made the other guys back up a little. The whole sky turned bright orange and blue as the sparks kept shooting out and up. Now we could see it all easy, those guys looked like they were pulling something out of those dark jackets they were wearing. In my head I thought they had to be guns.

"Get ready," Jimmy yelled, and he pulled the rocket from the straps that tied it to the case, and threw it at them. They jumped back like he had tossed a hand grenade. The roller skates slid out of the briefcase. Ripping the paper off the side of the case, he slid the wheels into the metal grooves. The Special Counterintelligence Mobile Unit was now ready for action.

"Go... Go..." Jimmy yelled at me, and started running to the other end of the yard. I was right behind. All at once the rocket exploded, and dark gray smoke gushed out all over the place. We couldn't see those guys on the other side, but they couldn't see us either. That's what we were hoping anyway. We were running with everything we had to the fence. Jimmy was carrying the briefcase, and I was pushing the bike. Windows were opening all up and down the street.

People were yelling out, asking what was going on. Only not being too nice the way they were asking. Heck, it was close to five in the morning. Then something happened that made me feel real good. Out of Jimmy's house, his Dad called out the window. His words weren't so nice either, but I sure was glad to hear them, and so was

Jimmy. Jimmy's dad wasn't talking to us though; don't even think he saw us. He was taking it out on the guys under his window. Don't think any of them were coming after us now; they were probably just trying to get back to their van. As the wind was blowing the smoke, I saw the guy on the ground finally push Ricky off of him. He went racing with his friends to get away. Me and Jimmy were at the fence now.

"What should we do," I wasn't sure.

"Gotta get your parents out!"

"Right!"

He heaved the case over the picket fence that was around that end of the garden. Then he helped me pick the bike up, and over it.

"To the Professor's place?" I asked.

"The Professor's place," he said. Then he handed me the briefcase when we got to the other side. "You're better on this," he said to me.

I jumped onto the briefcase, and Jimmy hopped on the bike. Together we started to roll down the street. When we hit the end near the intersection we heard screeching tires as the van pulled up behind us.

CHAPTER 6. THE CHASE

Suddenly, like out of nowhere, the van had speeded around the corner, the guys in black had come back after us. It was like a bad dream, 'cause it seemed like only seconds before that we had gotten rid of them, and no matter how fast we were running, they were always right behind us. It was like whoever the men in black were, they knew which way we were headed before we did. The van could've hit us, but it didn't. It was more like those guys wanted to catch us instead of kill us. Yet since we didn't know what their plans were for us, we just figured they wouldn't be something good, so we decided that even letting them catch us wasn't such a good idea.

Jimmy had a big lead, being he had the bike. My foot was shoving away the ground as fast as it could, but still couldn't keep up with him. They were breathing down our backs, my back mostly, but still the guys didn't bother to run us over. I would've been the first, since I was moving the slowest.

"They're getting too close," I yelled to Jimmy.

"Green Street," he called back to me.

Knew what that meant. Green Street was next street over, and most of the alleys in between the houses connected with Green Street. Since we played in this neighborhood all of our lives we knew just which one to pick. Had to find a good wide one to skate through.

All at once the van pulled right alongside of me. The window on the passenger side was open, and one of the men with his face still covered called to me.

"Pull over kid, or else!"

Didn't want to wait to find out what "or else," meant. The alley I was looking for was just two houses down from where I was. My foot pushed even harder against the street. Can't tell you how quick I was going on that thing. My heart was pumping so fast, that my lungs were burning just trying to keep up with it. In, out, in, out, the air just kept rushing through my mouth; and the sweat was pouring off of me, and mixing with the oil from the gas station. As it dripped down my face the mixture began to get into my eyes, and they started to sting. Didn't have time to think about that, 'cause I still had that nasty "or else" hanging over my head.

The alley I was gonna use was only one house away, when these guys stepped on the gas, and drove right in front of me. Couldn't stop the briefcase fast enough. Had to drop my foot extra hard, and pivot towards the curve. When my weight went back, the front end of the case went up in the air, and the wheels skipped up onto the curve. The back wheels followed with a hard thump, and I almost took a nosedive. So that I wouldn't fall, I leaped off of the case, and kept running alongside of it. It stopped when it hit the small wooden fence outside somebody's front lawn. In no time that guy that was riding shotgun, and I was really hoping he didn't have a shotgun; that guy jumped out of the front seat of the van, and was hot on my tail.

The van pulled right away from the curve, and was now going after Jimmy again. There was only one thing to do. Threw the case over the fence, and jumped over after it. The van speeded its way down the street, as that guy's footsteps were right behind me slapping against the sidewalk. I didn't bother looking back; I knew he was right behind me. I guess he didn't know how to be quiet when he was running at top speed. The shadow on the side of the wall let me know that he was reaching out to grab hold of me so, I zigzagged to try and dodge him. Guess he had played some football himself, 'cause he was right behind me, and the slap, slap, slap of his shoes against the ground seemed to be getting closer all the time. Then I began to cut across the lawn, and since there was only grass beneath my feet there was no place to hitch a ride on the briefcase.

The alley was at the side of the house, but that guy was running fast behind me. Didn't know if I could make it. If I did make it there wouldn't be anytime to set up the case. I'd have to run, and keep it going without stopping. Wanted to scream "HELP" at the top of my lungs, but if this mission was gonna stay secret, and save my parents; we couldn't let anybody know about what me and Jimmy were planning. The alley came up real soon. It was a tricky move, but what choice was the man in black giving me? His footsteps were almost on top of mine. I crouched down, and tossed the briefcase to the cement. It was rolling just ahead of me. With one gigantic leap my foot landed on top. My body wobbled a little, but somehow, I caught my balance. With two quick pushes the case, and me were speeding away. The footsteps kept up a little, but in a minute they stopped.

The walls of the alley were slim. My hands were stretched out to keep me from skidding into the sides of the houses. Now I was wondering how Jimmy had made out. Some streetlights up ahead told me that Green Street was just seconds away. What was gonna happen once I got there was something that really worried me. My heart was

111

pounding so fast and hard in my chest and head that I didn't think I could take much more.

Out on the street Jimmy was waiting for me. By going through another alley, he had beaten the van, but not by much. Around the corner came the speeding headlights doing ninety. They were at the other end of the block, but I didn't think they were gonna try and catch us this time. Not the way they were racing after us. This time they meant business, which meant if they caught up to us we were gonna get squashed.

"What now," I yelled to Jimmy, wanting the answer fast.

"Get them to slow down!"

"How?"

"Miller Street Drive, get on!"

Without asking why, I picked up the case, and jumped on the front bar right in front of Jimmy. Jimmy pushed off, and we were on our way.

Miller's Street Drive was just half a block away. It was kinda narrow, so I'm sure once they turned in there they'd have to slow down, but it wouldn't be enough to help us. Not anyway that popped into my head. Since Jimmy was the brains, and this was not the time to ask questions, I was just going along for the ride. Jimmy was standing on the pedals, pushing down as hard as he could. We were speeding along, but not nearly fast enough. The high beams of the van shined right onto the bike and us. Looked over my shoulder, but the light blinded my eyes.

"We're not gonna make it," I yelled.

Jimmy didn't answer; he just kept pumping the pedals as hard as he could. Miller's Street Drive was real close now, but the van was gaining ground too fast.

"NO!" I cried out. Couldn't hold that back.

Just as the van looked like it was gonna hit us, Jimmy, real quick like, spun the handlebars, and we skidded to the other side of the street. I almost fell off of the bike.

"Tell me when you're gonna do something like that," I yelled at him. It was a scare that I didn't need, and my heart really didn't need to be beating any faster.

The van went on by us, but the driver was pretty good, and had hit the brakes quick. The bike hit the pavement, and we popped up onto the curve. Being I was sitting on the hard metal, that move hurt me the most. My butt bounced off of the bar and back down again, hard. That's when Jimmy lost control of the bike, and we fell, sliding down on our sides.

The van had backed up real quick too. Jimmy had landed down all right, 'cause his feet touched down first. The bike wasn't hurt too bad but me; I was scrapped up and good. Couldn't tell if I was bleeding, didn't have time to care or to check it out. The van was already coming right at us. Jimmy grabbed me real fast by the arm, and pulled me up.

"The briefcase," I shouted and pointed. It was lying in the middle of the street. It was nearby, but I was wondering if it was nearby enough to take a chance on grabbing it up.

"Forget it," Jimmy shouted back.

The bike was up easy, and before the van could ram us we were rolling again, on the pavement, on the way to Miller Street Drive.

The van then pulled up onto the curb, and was chasing us down the sidewalk. They were coming up fast on us, but Miller Street Drive was real close now. Jimmy quickly steered the bike into the drive. The light beams seemed to be coming up real quick behind us.

"Here, you drive," Jimmy said.

"What?"

"Do it!"

So I did, while he peddled like a mad man, I steered like one.

"What are ya' doin'," I yelled, wondering why he was playing with the back of the bike.

"I'm gonna use the parachute," he yelled back.

"But that'll slow us down!"

"Trust me," he shouted, never looking back at me. And trusting Jimmy right then wasn't an easy thing to do with those headlights breathing down our necks, and letting us know that we were about to be squashed under the wheels of that speeding van. Suddenly Jimmy released the latch that held the chute in place. He fed the line out a little, and it caught the wind. The drag was slowing us down quick, just like I thought it would.

"What are you doing?" I screamed out.

Jimmy was too busy to answer; the van was just about to flatten us and the bike. There was a clicking sound, and Jimmy had released the chute, and it flew off the back of the bike, and onto the windshield of the van. Guess they couldn't see, 'cause the van steered away from us. By the sound of the brakes screeching, you could tell that they tried to stop, but couldn't do it before they crashed into the brick wall that lined the driveway. The horn was blasting. For guys on a secret mission they were sure making a lot of noise. They might have tried to come after us on foot, but we were long gone by then. Suddenly there was the sound of sirens coming in the distance. Even though we didn't want to run into the cops, I thought they sure took their good time getting there. Back around on Miller Street Drive I could hear the sound of the van revving up and screeching away. Guess they really didn't want to get caught by the police. As we whizzed along out onto the other street, I began to feel so happy, and started to laugh. Jimmy started laughing too. What a couple of nuts we sounded like. Don't know why we were laughing, we were still in deep trouble, just couldn't help it. My heart was pumping, and the blood was racing through my body making every part of me tingle. And my breath was still rushing in and out of me like it had no plans for slowing down any time soon. Between almost landing on the moon, and almost being crushed by that van, all I could do was feel the excitement. It was like I had been charged with electricity, and all I could do was feel the excitement and laugh. For that split-second, I had forgotten about my family, and the danger we were in. The wind was blowing by us at what seemed to be a hundred miles an hour. Jimmy slowed down on his laughing and said: "Now it's time!"

"Time for what?"

"Time to go back for the briefcase."

"Oh!"

"We're gonna be needing it."

Right then I stopped laughing, 'cause I remembered my parents were still with those men, and I remembered it wasn't over yet.

CHAPTER 7. DANGER IN THE WOODS

No, it wasn't over yet, that was for sure. This had sure been one crazy night, and outside of worrying about my parent's and my little sister it had been pretty cool. I'm saying that only because we were still alive, and had come out on top so far. That was no guarantee we that we were going to stay up there. A lot of what happened had only been good luck, which is as Jimmy pointed out, the only way to survive in the spy game but he said, "besides luck, you gotta have smarts." Jimmy sure had that. I guess it didn't hurt having old Ricky come bursting out of the house like the Calvary coming to the rescue either.

Like Jimmy thought, nobody was around when we showed up to pick up the briefcase. He figured that in all the commotion, nobody had noticed that we had dropped it. Still we were afraid, so when we went back for it, we never came to a full stop. Jimmy slowed up the bike, and I bent down, and swooped it up. After that it was full speed all the way back to the woods.

In the briefcase Jimmy had come ready for just about anything. There was a whole bunch of good stuff in there, like his Secret Bad Guy Deterrent No. 9. Which was mostly made up from old firecrackers and junk. Part of the Bad Guy Deterrent No. 9 package came with Bad Guy Blasters No. 7. Oh, good a new number, which were exploding darts that Jimmy had made, that blew up whenever they hit anything. Still don't know how he made most of this stuff. He had tested them all out before, and sometimes they even worked. The bad news was, that most of the time they didn't. When they did it was pretty nasty. Other stuff in there was a rope for climbing, a couple of water pistols loaded with color dye. I thought that they were just for messing around with other kids, but Jimmy told me that they were necessary for any mission of this magnitude. Using those big words always made Jimmy sound like he knew what he was talking about. Oh, and yeah, there was a book of matches. Guess that was for lighting the bombs, in case the lighter went out, and there was a bent-up cigarette, that Jimmy must have swiped from his Dad. Didn't know why he had that, far as I knew Jimmy didn't smoke, and the once he tried it got him sick as a dog. Smelled horrible, always wondered why someone would put that junk in their mouths. There was also some fishing line, don't know what that was for either and a flashlight. James Bond and Q Branch would have been proud. Q Branch were the guys who made all of James Bond's secret spy gadgets.

For most of the ride we stayed on a lot of back streets. Jimmy was going anyway, but the easy way to the Professor's lab. We had gone all the way around the edge of the town, and were going back to the woods another direction altogether. The wind was blowing hard, and we were starting to get a little cold, mainly because we were both covered in oil. Along the way Jimmy told me the plan. It was a good chance that whoever was chasing us would figure we'd head back to the lab, and maybe these guys already had the Professor, so we were gonna have to be extra careful.

When we got to the woods it was still pretty dark, but you could tell the sun was trying to get up from behind the trees. We took the bike as far as we could, before the ground got too bumpy, and then we had to hike the rest of the way.

The woods were still dark, and creepy enough to be scary that night, but darn everything was scary that night. Behind every tree I expected to find a bear, and there were snakes in those woods, and I hadn't spotted any snake poison medicine in Jimmy's briefcase. Even the clouds overhead were like out of horror movie, blocking the little bit of sunlight trying to make its way through. Every low hanging leaf became a deadly spider; every crunching twig trampled under my feet was a wolf out looking for a late-night snack. When a fallen branch had scratched at my leg, I was sure a poisonous viper had bitten me. I cried out, and Jimmy right away slapped his hand over my mouth, and he was right, I had to keep quiet, but my imagination was working real hard to turn the woods into the deadliest place on earth. And today with the men in black here, it might have been just that. Even the birds screeching in the trees made me think they might be giant vultures waiting to pick at our bones, after some killer bees had stung us to death in a deadly attack. I was beginning to wonder why I had ever come out to this place to play. You'd think there was enough real stuff to be worried about, that I didn't have to let my imagination give me a whole bunch of new junk to be afraid of. We hadn't really gone too far when Jimmy stopped me.

"Wait," he said," and he opened the briefcase, and took out one of the squirt guns. Then he pointed it at my face. "Close your eyes."

"What are you gonna do," I squinted.

"Ricky licked all the oil off of your face, you're gonna be too easy to see."

"Aw, man!"

"It ain't gonna hurt!"

"It's getting light out."

"Not light enough yet."

"Put it on your hand first, then rub it in so ya' don't shoot me in the eye." My eyes were still stinging from the oil that had already gotten into them. If I couldn't see, that would make it real hard to dodge a stampede of wild moose, or whatever other danger was waiting for us in those woods.

"Good idea." And he did it. Then he rubbed a little on himself just to make sure he was still hard to see in the dark.

Guess we were starting to feel the cold even more, because the early morning breeze was really starting to creep in. Before, there wasn't a time or a chance to notice the chill coming on, but now as we were walking it started to sneak up on us. There were still other things on my mind, but my teeth were chattering together just the same. Hoped it was the cold making them do that, but it never left my head that there were other reasons for my teeth to be tap dancing in my mouth.

It was still kinda dark, and making it hard to make our way through all the trees. If we had gone our regular way, finding the lab would've been a breeze, but going in the back way in the dark made it rough. It still seemed like night with the daylight trying to creep its way in. For that reason, we wanted the sun to shine through a little more, then again we didn't. The sun could be our friend, shinning just enough light to guide us through the trees, or in the last-minute turn on us, and let us be seen by the enemy, the men in black.

After a little bit I stopped to ask Jimmy, "Do ya' know where we're goin'?"

"Should be close by now."

"But I don't know this place, not in the dark."

"It should be close..."

"Why don't ya' use the flashlight?"

"We got a little bit of the sun coming up!"

"There ain't that much sun, and I still don't know this place. The moon's gone, and it wasn't helping much when it was shining full blast over our heads," I told him.

"If we use the flashlight, they might see us comin'."

"And if we don't use it, we might never find the lab."

When I talked to Jimmy, I sounded a little mad, but my parents and my little sister were still back home with some guys dressed up all in black. Guys who had tried to run us over, and that was making me kinda nervous. I think Jimmy knew why I was acting the way I was, 'cause he stopped arguing with me, and went along with what I was saying.

"Yeah, okay," he said, and he felt around in the case for the flashlight. "Got it," and he pulled it out.

"We'll just keep it pointed at the ground, so it'll be hard to see."

That was all right by me. The light wasn't much help, 'cause all the trees still looked the same. Yet it made me feel better having it on. At least I'd be able to see any deadly snakes crawling through the dirt.

In the dark, it seemed like we had walked an awful long time. If Jimmy knew the way, we should've been there by now. Still all my complaining wouldn't help any, so finally I did shut my trap. I was still thinking, thinking too much. We were both walking with our hands in front of our face, and looking through our spread-out fingers, so we didn't crash into anything with our heads, or get jabbed in the eye by a low hanging branch. We got to a spot where all the trees clumped together. We had a tough time getting through there. In some places we had tried to go through, and we had to come out, and go around another way. The branches were scratching us something terrible, and every time I'd let loose with an "ouch" Jimmy would warn me to "shut up." I didn't know why he wasn't "ouching" himself. He had to be getting torn apart by those branches.

"What am I supposed to do, I'm hurtin' I whispered.

"Shhh!"

"I whispered, so go shhh yourself, you got us lost in here and…"

"Will you shut up?" Yeah, already I was starting to complain all over again.

"Let's just call the police, I'm really afraid for my Mom and Dad!" I was starting to get more upset and more scared than ever, and that's the main reason I was mad at Jimmy.

"That's not a good idea, I told ya'."

"Yeah, that's what you told, me, but…"

"Shhh!"

"Stop tellin' me to..."

"Trust me..."

"No, I don't trust..." That's all I got out when the flashlight switched off. "What's wrong," I said first thing.

"I heard something."

"Don't play games with me Jimmy."

"This ain't game playing time Shawn," he said real low, and then he put his arm on my shoulder, and spoke like the good friend I knew he was. "Your Mom and Dad, your sister are in trouble, this ain't no time to fool around. We're their only chance, that's what I really think."

"But we're just kids," I moaned, guess I sounded like a little kid too.

"Yeah, we're kids now, but if we can get our hands on the Gravity Boxes, we'll be more than just kids, we'll be something bigger then all of them put together. Then we can get your parents out safe."

My eyes looked at him long and hard, at what was mostly just a dark outline, but what he said made sense.

"Trust me," he asked me again, "please." Since Jimmy was my only chance, and since he was the smartest guy I knew, and my best friend, I decided to do just that.

With the flashlight out, and the sky turning from black to gray, we both just listened. In a moment I heard it too. It was the sound of twigs crunching, and it was getting louder. Both me and Jimmy ducked down to keep an eye out for whatever it was coming towards us. Then we saw it. Three of the guys in black coming right our way.

Couldn't make out much more, except there were three of them. Jimmy didn't have to tell me to shut up this time. That was something we both knew to do. From my earlier teaming with Jimmy in the spy business, I knew that if we just sat quiet and didn't move, they'd probably never notice us. In the dark if they did see us squatting, we might just look like rocks or something. It was starting to get lighter out now, so that wasn't good. The important thing was not to move, not an inch. Staying still when you absolutely had to be was a very hard thing to do. I was holding my breath, and I don't think Jimmy was breathing either, and no they didn't see us, 'cause they kept talking, as the guys in black got nearer.

"We've got to finish this all off tonight," said one of them.

"What about those kids," said another one.

"We'll find them, don't worry about that," the first guy said.

"But if we don't..." said the second guy.

"It's got to be finished off tonight."

"We're running out of night," the second one came back at him.

The third guy hadn't said anything, as they passed by. We waited a little longer without moving, and then Jimmy talked first.

"More good news!"

"What do ya' think they meant finish everything off?"

"You don't want know what I think."

"I hate it when you talk like that!"

"Guess I was wrong!"

"What do ya' mean?"

"When we saw those guys at your house, I started to think that maybe this hadn't been the beginning of their mission."

"Huh?"

"They already knew something about us, where you lived…"

"Then…"

"Then the first time we saw those guys, just looked like the beginning of something, like they were gonna start spying on the Professor. What we saw was the end of their operation. They weren't putting in a bug; they were taking one out. They didn't want to leave any trace behind that they had been there. They've probably been watching the Professor, and even us for a long time now."

When Jimmy said that, a chill ran up my spine. Probably for the millionth time that night I shook like ice water had been thrown in my face. And this time it definitely wasn't from the cold. To think that somebody had been really spying on me, and I never even knew it really bothered me. Sometimes Jimmy being so smart was a real pain, 'cause that was something that I'd rather not have known about.

"So what now," I said, really afraid of knowing the answer.

"We have to go on."

"But those guys know all about us," still didn't want to believe that. "They know about all our spy stuff. They know everything!"

"But we're kids," Jimmy reminded me, and I didn't know why he was saying that, when that had been my argument all night.

"But I thought you said…?"

"Let's use us being kids against them."

"Huh?"

"They won't take us seriously. They'll think because we're kids, it was all stupid stuff, that we just got lucky, that it's all going to be easy for them."

"But..."

"And then we'll show them what kids can do!"

I could tell he was serious and determined. And you didn't want to get in Jimmy's way when he got like that.

"Trust me," he said again. I spent a few seconds looking at the shadow in front of his face. "Well?"

"What choice do I have?"

"Good," he answered, "we've got to really move now, the sun's comin' up fast. Got another half hour at the most of darkness to cover us, and that's gonna be mostly shadows."

"How we gonna find the Professor's place, we're still not sure which way."

"That's easy now!"

"How?"

"We just follow the guys in black. They can only be headed one place."

CHAPTER 8. RESCUE AT THE LAB.

From there on in we never turned on the flashlight. Since the men were still walking heavy, making noise I mean, Jimmy was right. They were taking us right to the lab. The problem with that was, we had to stay back pretty far, and walk light on our toes so they didn't notice us. We really couldn't see them anymore, just hear the crunching sounds they made treading over all the leaves, and fallen branches, and junk. Me and Jimmy weren't doing much talking, none in fact. Didn't want them to hear us yapping either. It was terrible though. Even trying to be quiet, every step sounded as loud as anything, and seemed to echo through the trees, especially, 'cause we knew they were real close by. Lot of that was in my imagination, I guess, but still scary. Had to slow down a couple a times, 'cause we thought we were being too loud, but couldn't go too slow, or we'd lose them altogether. Must have been like Jimmy said, we were kids, so they didn't expect too much from us. Never thought we'd be right on their tail. Probably thought any sounds they heard were chipmunks or birds, not two super spies just a little ways behind them.

All at once like, the crunching stopped. Right away Jimmy put his hand on my chest to stop me too. Guess he noticed it first. For a long time we didn't do nothing, just stood there quiet like.

"Wait here," Jimmy whispered, and he moved as slow as possible a few feet ahead. He stopped, waited a minute, and then came back the same way. "The lab's right up ahead," he said keeping his voice real low. "Saw the lights from behind that tree. That's why they stopped making noise."

"How'd they do that?"

"Probably trained a real long time, like Ninjas or something."

"They're good aren't they," I hated to ask, 'cause I already knew the answer.

"Real good," Jimmy said, and he wasn't happy about it either. "They got the Professor, you're Mom, Dad, and sister, and before they leave they plan to have us too. You heard them yourself. So we don't got any choice."

"But they're good you said."

"Maybe too good."

"What do you mean?"

"They underestimated us once before. Maybe they won't do it again."

"But we're kids," I knew he would understand what I meant.

"Then again, like I said, they might think we're two dumb kids that just got lucky. Anyway, we got surprise on our side."

Jimmy was right, who would be out in those creepy woods in the dark, not even two dumb kids.

"I'd rather have a dozen of Green Berets."

"All we got to do is get our hands on them gravity machines, and we can beat these guys."

"Yeah, well the problem with that is, if they got the Professor, they probably got the machines."

"Well we got a plan, right?"

"Guess so."

To tell the truth, I wasn't exactly thrilled to death with this plan. Each time we were getting closer and closer to getting caught. But Jimmy was right about one thing. These guys sure sounded serious about getting their hands on us, so now it was just a matter of getting our hands on the Gravity Boxes first. Just waiting around our time was sure to run out.

The both of us moved over behind a large tree to get a better look at the lab. As Jimmy edged ahead a little more, the hand holding the briefcase bumped against the tree. He almost let go with an ouch himself, but was able to hold most of it in. The men walking suddenly stopped. They looked around for a long minute. Jimmy backed up behind the tree, and just held his breath. The birds were starting to chirp in the trees real loud. The men stopped and listened, and then went into the Professor's place. This time they had just walked in the side door uninvited. Passing in front of the window we saw another man meet them coming in.

"You almost made my heart stop man," I told him.

"Keep it down", he whispered, kinda upset back at me. Then we saw another one of the men in black. "Darn, there's another one," Jimmy said. "How many of those guys are there?"

"You're thinking there might be more?"

"Maybe."

"Stop agreeing with me," About that, I really wanted both of us to be guessing wrong.

"They most likely left the lights on, 'cause they're out in the middle of the woods, not expecting anyone to see."

"Thought they were expecting us."

"Maybe not, maybe they're thinking we'd head for the police station."

"Or I gotta worse idea."

"Let's hear it. It can't be any worse than what I'm thinking." Jimmy was more into hearing my scary thoughts, than I was into hearing his.

"Well I'm not really trying to top ya', but just the same you're not gonna like it."

"Name one thing I've liked about running into these guys?"

"Suppose they wanted us to come back, so they leave the lights on. Make it look like they're not waiting for us."

"And…"

"This is the part you're not gonna like."

"Come on, spill it."

"What's out there," and I pointed to some of the trees. "Maybe they got other guys in black waiting for us."

"But…"

"Like ya' said, we ain't got no choice. We'd have to try for the Gravity Boxes, maybe they'd know that too."

"Beautiful Shawn," and he almost sounded happy about my brilliant thinking. And what I was thinking did nothing, but make me shake in my cold oil-soaked sneakers even more.

"Hey what about the police station?"

"Maybe put guys there too, who knows how many they got? Only one thing bothering me…"

"Just one thing?"

"Why'd they start walking quiet if they already had the Professor?"

"Yeah why would they,.."

Jimmy cut me off. "Got it! Maybe they thought we'd already be around, and if we were close by..."

"I get it," I said.

Jimmy put his head down, which meant that he was thinking. I was doing pretty good in the thinking department myself that night. Maybe being dropped from the clouds could do that for a kid. But when Jimmy put on the thinking cap, and got to thinking really deep, that usually meant something crazy and dangerous was gonna pop out of his brain. After a minute, just like I thought, it did.

"Here's what we do..." he started to tell me. It all sounded nuts, but so did soaring through the sky holding onto a flying box, and getting chased by spies. The plan was simple. First thing we had to do was get anyone near the house to look the other way. When they were looking one way, we had to be somewhere else. Jimmy explained that it was like doing a magic trick, the magician always made the audience look somewhere else when he was tricking them.

So, here's what we did. Jimmy set a bunch of his firecrackers along the ground. Then he took a piece of string, and rubbed it on the oil on his stomach. When it was good and greasy, he tied it to the fuses of the firecrackers. Then he took the pack of matches and the cigarette out of the case.

"Was wonderin' why you carried that around."

"You'll see."

Our Dad's would have killed us if they saw us with cigarettes. Well maybe not kill us, but it would have been bad.

He started to light the cigarette, but the first puff made him almost choke his brains out.

"Shhh." It was me telling him to be quiet for the first time that night. He was having real trouble stopping the coughing, so he covered his mouth with his hand, and pushed the cigarette at me, so I could give it a try.

"Ah man, I ain't any good at this." But he kept choking, and pushing the cigarette at me. Didn't have any chance to say no. After lighting the match, I tried not to get any of the smoke down my throat, 'cause that's what had made Jimmy start hacking up a lung. After a couple of puffs, the end got red, and it was lit. By then Jimmy had stopped choking, and could talk again.

"What's this for," I asked again.

"Watch, I'll show you." Then somehow, he turned all this junk into a time bomb.

"This is my Special Tactical Distraction Device Number…" he started to say.

"Number nine," I cut him off.

He looked at me annoyed for a second, and then he continued. "When it burns down it'll light the string, and that will set the firecrackers off."

"You mean it's a fuse…"

Once more he looked annoyed at me, and then he went on. "That gives us just enough time to get to the other side of the lab.

Since the firecrackers are all in a line, they'll get a bunch of explosions instead of one big one."

"Sounding like gun fire."

"That's what I hope they'll think, and where are a couple of dumb kids gonna get guns?"

"Do ya' think it will work?"

"I'm hoping, I'm really hoping."

"Me too, "I said.

"Come on, we gotta make a wide circle to get to the other side, just in case they got people watching."

Then we started to run. The sun was a little higher now, and you could see it shinning through the clouds and the tall trees. In no time we'd be pretty easy to see, especially with the blue dye all over our faces. But they'd be easy to see too dressed all in black. We made it around to the far side of the house pretty quick. Jimmy kept the briefcase and everything with him. Now we had to wait for the first explosion.

"It ain't doin' nothin'," I said not knowing if that was a reason to be happy or not, 'cause I was really scared about what we were gonna to do after.

"It'll go," Jimmy promised.

"But what if..."

"Enough of what ifs, we're spies, we gotta think positive!"

"But we're just..."

"And don't say we're just kids again. Being kids ain't any good right now. We gotta be spies. It's just important that they think we're only kids. Listen, I know there ain't much of a chance of it working. They're grown men, real trained secret agents or Ninjas, they probably have guns, but if we don't at least act as if we can pull this off, then we're dog meat for sure."

I nodded to let him know that I understood. Was so scared, but knew we didn't have no choice.

"Here..." he said, and real quick Jimmy took a out a couple of the Ultra Secret Projectiles... Actually, I couldn't remember the name Jimmy had given this one, but you had to be real careful with them. "Before I forget, and don't bump the tips." He handed them to me with some of the fishing line. "And take one of these while you're at it," then he gave me one of the water pistols with the dye.

"What am I supposed to do with that?" I asked him.

"Who knows, but you might think of something."

So real fast I stuck the darts in the back of my pants, and the water pistol in the front. The fishing line slipped right into my pocket. Still there was no explosion. I think Jimmy was getting a little nervous, 'cause out of nowhere he said, "Don't worry, its gonna go blow any second." I could tell the way he said it that he wasn't really sure.

"Cigarettes without somebody puffing on them burn pretty slow," I told him.

"Yeah, that's right," he said, sounding glad to have me agreeing with him.

We didn't have to wait much longer, after a few more seconds the loud blast boomed from across the woods. We looked right away at the house, but nothing happened. No one moved outside, and no one came out to see what the noise was. So far there had only been one firecracker blow up.

"What happened to the other…" That's all I got out when everything went nuts. Firecrackers started exploding all over the place. We watched the house another minute, and then from out of nowhere we see this guy dart out from behind a tree. Neither of us had seen him before. Then another guy came running through the door with two others following him. He must've been the boss, 'cause he started shouting out orders to everybody else.

"Get out there, and find those kids. NOW!"

We hadn't fooled them for long. Just then we saw two other guys run from behind trees, and heading for where the firecrackers were exploding.

"Now," Jimmy pushed me towards the house.

Next thing I know, we're both running at the house. There was nobody left on the porch. That was our sign to go. We had to hope that all of the agents were out looking for us, and distracted enough by the firecrackers not to look back. How many more were inside, and what were we gonna do when we got there? These were things we had talked about, but it all seemed so impossible as we ran to the far side of the house. It seemed like we could make it there easy and not be seen, but only if more of those real spies weren't hiding behind other trees. We made it as fast as we could. When we got to the house, me and Jimmy edged around to the side of the wooden porch, and threw the briefcase under it, and then he dove under right after. I did the same. Only thing wrong with that action was landing on the water pistol.

"Owww," started to come out of my mouth, but Jimmy's hand slapped me across my lips right away. That only made me hurt worse, 'cause my teeth banging against his hand cut the inside of my mouth. But I was just scared enough not to pay attention to any of it. "What now," I whispered.

"We stick to our plan," he whispered back to me.

"But there's more of them then we thought!"

"I got us this far, didn't I?"

Yeah, Jimmy really had done that. He's gotten us right into the middle of a really bad situation, where we were probably gonna get killed, so how could I ever thank him. That was easy to do; just keep my trap shut. And that was easy too, 'cause those guys dressed in black were already coming back, and like I thought there were more of them, lots more. And I couldn't think of any better reason to keep my lips zippered, 'cause now danger really was our business.

CHAPTER 9. WHAT WOULD JAMES BOND DO.

From beneath the porch, we peeked from behind the wooden beams that held it up, and could see just the feet of the guys that were now searching around the house, searching for us. Had a terrible feeling where they were gonna look next. Me and Jimmy crawled back as far as we could under the house. It was all wet and muddy back there, but with all the oil and ink all over me, it really didn't seem worth complaining about.

The sky was getting much lighter now, so we tried to bury ourselves in the shadows under the porch. Jimmy must've been thinking the same as me. He tapped me on the shoulder, and when I looked at him, he started pushing up clumps of the soft dirt and mud into a pile in front of him. He was using the side of the briefcase like a plow. Guess he wanted me to do the same, so that's what I did, and I had only my hands to work with. We were moving kinda fast, but still didn't want to make any noise. The soft dirt began to look like a small hill, and he real quick like made another pile right next to it, so that they made one long mountain of mud. Then with the case he pressed against it, so that dirt would stay packed.

There were a lot of feet trampling around on the outside. Maybe not all that many, but it sure seemed like there were a lot of them. Guess it was better they were making a little noise, so that we could hear them now.

Jimmy was just ready to start helping me pack in my little pile of dirt, when we heard some feet stomping onto the porch that was just over us. We froze when we heard their voices.

"Out here," one of them asked. "Check out everything."

"But..."

"They got to be somewhere; they didn't just disappear."

"Yes Sir!"

Then one pair of feet ran off of the porch, and landed on the ground stirring up the dirt right in front of us, and my heart jumped with the sound of those boots hitting down. And now the pounding of my heart and the burning in my lungs were going nuts, just like when I was being chased through the streets by these guys. Only this time, I wasn't running, my body was just frozen in the mud under that old porch. I covered my mouth with my hands, and buried my face deeper into the dirt to keep the gasp from escaping out into the open.

"Down," Jimmy said, in a real low voice, but excited like, and dove behind his mud pile, but I had already beat him to the punch, and now I was just trying not to choke on the dirt pressed against my face. With my one eye sticking out of the mud, I could see the feet in front of the porch suddenly turn around, and point in our direction. Jimmy grabbed my head and pulled me. I looked up quick, and right away I knew what the problem was. My head was pressed to the dirt, but my butt was still up in the air, so I flattened out quick like behind my pile of dirt. The only problem with that was, my little hill wasn't altogether built yet. From behind a tiny valley of mud you could see this guys knees begin to bend. Our worst fear was about to come true, he was gonna look under the porch. Without even thinking about it, I

138

mashed my whole body into the mud again. I had slurped down a lot of dirt that night, so I guessed that extra pound I had just swallowed couldn't hurt much. If only the ink and oil looked enough like the dirt, then maybe he wouldn't see me. All I could think about was that my one leg was still out in the open with nothing hiding it. That old Ninja trick popped into my head again, and I became like a rock. What didn't move was harder to see, that was the way it flashed into my head. If I was still enough, this guy might believe that I was just some old rock that was sitting under the house.

With my eyes shut tight, the flashlight that was shining under the porch made everything seem red as it passed over my head. Didn't want to breathe either. Rocks don't do that. That was part of the secret of becoming a rock. After the first time the light passed, I thought it was all over.

Then it came by again, and I thought it was gonna stop right on me, 'cause my head was still sticking out a little. Without me telling them to my eyes started to open, but I caught them just in time, and kept them squeezed tight. Then that fast the light and the guy were gone. Me and Jimmy still kept frozen for a long time, 'cause right then and there being under that old porch seemed a whole lot better than being out in the open, and playing chase with the guys in black. Think it was me who moved first. My hand nudged the top of Jimmy's head. He stuck his face up to look at me. We both let go of a mouth full of air. It felt like we'd been holding our breaths for hours. I knew it wasn't that long, but it seemed like we had our faces buried in dirt forever.

Those other guys sounded like they were a little further away, but just far enough so that we could talk, just not too loud. From there on in we were both whispering everything we said.

"That was too close," I said first.

"You're tellin' me," the sound of his voice told me that Jimmy was shook too, like that wasn't something I didn't already know.

"Could swear that light shinned right on my face."

"Well I'd have been caught too," and he said it like he thought I was blaming him or something.

"No, I just meant," I tried to get out.

"What would James Bond do," he stopped me real quick with that one. "How would he get out of this?"

"He would pull out his forty-five, and go to town on these guys."

"James Bond doesn't carry a forty-five. He uses a Beretta."

"Yeah, but then he got a…"

"Forget about it, we don't have one of them either," Jimmy's voice became a little louder when he came back with that. Who could believe that he was thinking about this stuff now?

"But you…"

"Shhh," that was becoming Jimmy's favorite word. He was right of course our whispers were getting a little too loud. "We got to get into the house, that's what we gotta do."

"He'd sneak up on them."

"What?"

"James Bond!"

"Oh!"

"And knock 'em out."

"We're not ready for that!"

"Good, I'm glad. How we gonna do it?"

"Do what?"

"Get into the house?"

"Oh!"

It was me that decided to pay attention to what he was talking about, 'cause no way was he listening to me.

"How we gonna do it?"

"We're gonna have to take a chance."

"So what else is new?" Like what had we been doing all night and into the day?

"This will be our moment of maximum risk."

We'd been having those maximum risk moments since last night too, but I think he meant that's when we were most likely to get shot. So I think that's what I didn't like about the plan.

"First we gotta check to see if those guys are still off in the woods looking for us." Jimmy said. "My guess is that some of them are, since they didn't find us around the house."

"You're guessin'!"

"Most likely anyway." It was sounding better all the time, not really. "So if we get out of here soon, we got a good chance of hitting the back door, and breezing in that way." Somehow now we were just gonna breeze in the back door. Then he started to crawl to the side of the porch.

"Wooo," I called him back.

"What?"

"Got more questions," Didn't really, but I wanted to get it all straight in my head before we charged out into the open. Then again, maybe I just was putting this whole breezing in thing off as long as I could.

"Like what?"

"Ah... what if the doors locked?"

"It ain't."

"How do you know?"

"Because, if you were listening, only the screen door slammed shut, and there's no lock on that." It killed me when he was so smart.

"What if somebody's in the kitchen?"

"You're stalling." Which was true, 'cause we were about to hit that moment of maximum risk, AGAIN! Like this was gonna be worse than all of the other junk that happened since last night. Part of me didn't even believe that was possible, but there I was stuck in the mud, covered in oil, with lots of bad guys hunting us down with guns, so I was stalling a bit.

"But what if..."

"You're stalling" Jimmy cut me off again, he wasn't gonna let me get any of questions out, and right then my questions were the only thing between us and our "moment maximum of risk".

"Somebody in the kitchen?"

"That's another chance we're gonna have to take. If we get that far, there's a good shot we can get to the closet and that one gravity machine."

"That's two chances too many."

That's when Jimmy gave me a good hard stare. It was still dark under that porch, but I could feel his eyes drilling holes through me.

"You coming," he said.

"Might as well," I told him.

"Know how to use your darts?"

"What do we need to? Just throw them like a regular dart."

"You got it, and make sure you ain't close when it goes off."

"This is crazy," I said, and it was, it really was.

"Yeah, I know, but right now being crazy is our business," Jimmy came back at me. Through the shadows I could see he was trying to smile, but I could tell he was just as scared as me. Then he said the scariest words I had heard since all this craziness started, "Let's go!"

And he was right again. If there was any shot of saving my family, or even ourselves, we had to get to those Gravity Boxes. We were desperate, and desperation, as Jimmy would say: "Can make people do incredibly brave, or incredibly stupid things. The secret was to try and not be too stupid." I always had the feeling that he was talking right at me when he added the last part. But how could we stay smart, and still be charging into a house filled with spies, or deadly Ninjas, or whatever those guys were. And maybe the house wasn't filled with spies, but I was sure that the guys in black wouldn't leave the house unguarded. What was inside was too important.

Then we crawled from under the porch. First, Jimmy sneaked a look to see if anyone was out there. He pushed me back a little when this one guy came out of the woods. Like earthworms we slithered back into the mud again, and like a second later the guy walked right on by us, and around to the side of the house. That was our chance, maybe our only chance. There was no one else in sight, and no noise coming from the porch right overhead. In no time they'd start coming back, and looking closer to the house again, so it was now, or wait 'til dark to make our move. With my parent's and my little sister being held prisoners back at the house, being scared wasn't a good enough reason not to go anymore. I thought about it a second, didn't have to think too hard, 'cause if anything happened to them, I didn't care what happened to me anyway.

Once out from under the porch, we moved fast. Using our hands, we sprung up on to the deck. So far nobody was around. Like Jimmy had said, the back door was opened. It screeched a little when we went into the kitchen. Made sure it closed nice and easy, we still didn't know how close anyone was. We only took a few steps, when from the living room we could hear some voices, but couldn't make out what they were saying. Me and Jimmy ducked into the hallway, so they wouldn't see us. I looked down at the floor, and pointed out to Jimmy the mud and grease tracks we had just left behind. He just shrugged his shoulders, 'cause there didn't seem to be anything that we could do about that. Just had to hope that the bad guys were too busy doing evil things to notice. Jimmy pointed to his exploding dart, and then pulled one out. I did the same.

"Just in case," he whispered in my ear. That's when we started tiptoeing. He was leading me to the door that went down to the basement. There we could hide 'til the voices stopped.

When the men left the living room, it would be clear sailing to the lab and the second box, which we hoped they didn't know about yet. Jimmy remembered, that we had only talked about that second Gravity Box outside of the lab. So maybe the bugs didn't pick up on the fact that there was a second box. We were moving really quiet now. Jimmy slowly turned the handle to the door. Good, it didn't make any noise. As the door began to open, all we could see was the dark at the bottom of the steps. That meant nobody was down there. WRONG! When the light switched on, a hand came out of nowhere, and grabbed hold of Jimmy. He screamed out; 'cause he got scared, we both did. The briefcase dropped to the floor.

All at once I could see this guy coming out of the basement like some kinda demon rising from the darkness, and grabbing hold of Jimmy. It was a trap, and he had been standing on the stairs all the time waiting for us. Now this big guy lifted Jimmy into the air like he was picking up a baby, and held him so tight that he couldn't move, except to kick his legs around wild like. But even when Jimmy's kicking feet hit the guy they just bounced off like a ball bouncing off a wall. Jimmy yelled out, "let me go! Let me go!" I wasn't thinking fast enough, so Jimmy reminded me: "The dart, the dart," he shouted.

Just as soon as I got over being in shock, and could think of what to do, my right hand with the dart in it came up over my head. Swear I was gonna throw it right at this guy, but before I could even take aim, somebody grabbed hold of me too from behind. The dart fell to the floor, but did not explode. Me and Jimmy, we put up a good fight, but these two guys were like animals, and were a heck of a lot bigger and stronger. Like a second later a bunch of their friends showed up, held us by our legs and arms, and took us right to the ground. Now we weren't going any place.

"Let me go," Jimmy yelled at them again, but they weren't listening.

"Bring them in the other room," another man said, who had just come in from the lab. Guess he was the boss. Before they did that, they rolled each of us over on our stomachs, and slipped something that looked like plastic garbage ties over our wrist. Now our hands were tied behind our backs. It cut a little, and I let loose with an "Owww," I cried out, but they didn't say nothing, or try to loosen it for me. Then they lifted us by our arms, and that hurt too. These guys were treating us kinda rough, and pretty much handling us like the garbage bags that went with the ties.

Once up on our feet, they really didn't give us a chance to walk, but dragged us along the rug into the living room. In there they sat us down hard on the Professor's rug. Now without their black hoods on, we could see what they looked like. They were all big, and mean looking, and I thought being so ugly might have been the reason that they wore those hoods over their heads. The one doing all the talking looked the meanest. A tall blond haired guy, with nasty looking eyes, that seemed to be looking right through us, and there was a scar running down his left cheek. He was a big brute; you know the kind super spies always tangled with. None of them had taken off their gloves. Guess they didn't want to leave any fingerprints lying around. So that meant to me that they didn't care if we saw what they looked like, 'cause they had us now, and there was no way we were gonna rat on them. Jimmy must've figured that out in his head too. Maybe I was wrong, and really hoping I was.

"The parachute," said the guy I thought was the boss, "That was good, very good." Then he picked up one of the darts, and touched the head real easy like, and looked at us. "Exploding darts," he said.

"Why don't you smack it against your head and see," Jimmy told him nasty like.

Go Jimmy, I thought, 'cause I was too scared to be cocky. The man smiled, but it wasn't a friendly smile, more like he was just enjoying having us helpless on the floor in front of him.

"Very good," the blond guy said, "in a couple of years you might have gotten away with it, although you would, I suspect, have been too interested in girls to be a problem."

"Whaddya do with my Mom, and Dad, and sister," I yelled to him.

I said it kinda loud, and he looked like he was annoyed with my question, so he didn't answer, but just kept talking about what he wanted to. He picked up the briefcase, and was gonna open it, when he said, "Its not going to explode on me, is it?"

"Why don't you open it, and see for yourself," Jimmy said.

The tall blond man smiled again, and said, "I like this kid." Then he sat the case in front of Jimmy, and flipped open the latches, so that it would open towards Jimmy's face. Jimmy didn't move an inch.

"I don't think so," said the man, and then he opened it all the way and looked inside.

147

"Good, very good," he said, and then he closed it up, and put it on the coffee table. "You see," he went on, "after that trick with parachute, we knew we were dealing with two very smart boys. You could possibly make it all the way into the house. Which is exactly what we wanted you to do. You were smart, but not smart enough to figure that out. We didn't underestimate our opponents, and neither should have you. Outside there was too much space to cover. You could hide behind trees, or rocks, or there could also be another rocket blasting flare, which was also very good." He said it like he was congratulating us. "We are a small band" he went on, "and a search of the entire forest would have been impossible. You were correct in not going to the police; we would have been waiting for you. And even if you called them, let's just say we have friends in the police department. We like to cover all our bases, but in the end, I figured that you would come back here. There was only one hope of defeating us, and that is now gone. Me and Jimmy just looked at each other; it really looked like the end of us, and probably my parents, and sister too.

"So, the ideal thing to do, was to make it possible to get into the house, but not too easy", the blond guy kept talking. "That would have set off all sorts of alarms in your head for smart boys like you. Once inside the house, that would make it simple, and of course you cooperated splendidly." He smiled at us. "Thinking back, and you might agree, you should have just kept running. All that would have given you was a little extra time, but now even that has run out."

"What did you do with my do with my Mom and Dad, and little sister," I asked again. He could tell I was mad and upset too.

"So, you were going to rescue Professor Burkhardt, and get him to help you... and just how was he going to do that," and he said it like he really didn't know. Jimmy looked at me, and shook his head real hard. "It doesn't matter," the man said, like he didn't care. "Soon we are going to know everything."

"What about my family?" Felt like crying again, 'cause it really worried me. Still that creep wouldn't answer me.

"You wanted to go to the basement, and I agree that was a good choice," he said, then he told a couple of the other guys: "Bind their feet, and make sure they don't make a lot of noise. Lay them on the basement floor, we don't want them getting the Professor's furniture all greasy." He smiled again, 'cause he knew they really had us this time. One thing I hate worse than a bad loser, is a bad winner.

"But my parents," that's all I could get out when one of them took some tape, and wrapped it around my mouth.

"At least tell him about his parents," Jimmy tried to get out for me, but they weren't letting him say anything either. His mouth was wrapped shut too. Then another plastic tie, a bigger one, was wrapped around my legs and Jimmy's too. The trip to the basement was the worst I'd ever taken. We were both being carried by two guys each. One had our arms, and the other had our legs. The way they handled us really hurt, 'cause they used my arms to pick me up, and the plastic ties around my feet were used like a handle. It cut into my ankles, but there was no way to tell them that with the tape stuck across my mouth. Like they would have cared. Carrying us down the steps, they bounced us up and down, and that made the cuts hurt worse. Maybe I was even bleeding, but I couldn't see my wrists that were tied behind me. All I could do was feel the pain.

We were put right onto the floor, just like they were told to do. Even though it was hot out, the cement floor down in the basement was freezing cold. Couldn't do much else, but look each other in the eye. I don't think Jimmy looked as sad as me, but that's all we could do before the lights went out.

CHAPTER 10. WHEN DANGER REALLY BECAME OUR BUSINESS.

Jimmy kept saying it, "danger is our business." Maybe it was him saying it so much that made it really our business. Because tied up there on that cold cement, I knew we were really in bad trouble, and for some reason, I was blaming him in my head for making it all come true. If only he hadn't kept saying it, I thought. Know that sounds stupid, but that's the way I felt. It's like he was wishing for it to happen, and somehow that was the reason that spies had come to the Professor's place, that my parents and little sister were in danger, and that I was there on that cold floor shaking with my teeth chattering. Then I thought no, Jimmy's not like that. He likes a little excitement like me, but what was happening was a lot more than even he'd be wishing for. It wasn't like before, with the parachute and all, I wasn't feeling good after meeting with these guys the second time. It was making me pretty scared, more than even when I thought I was gonna go crashing into that airplane with the second Gravity Box. Scared for me and for my family. But with all this coming down, it kept popping in my head, if only Jimmy hadn't said those words, "danger is our business", none of this would have happened.

It was cold on that floor, like I told ya'. Even with the lights turned off, there was some light from the sun coming in through the window that was up over our heads. It was a pretty dirty window, so there wasn't all that much sunlight making it easier to see.

Me and Jimmy, well we just kept looking at each other. It wasn't easy with that junk still all over our faces, and the only light coming through that dusty old window. We were both just thinking, and who knew just how much time we had left for that?

Goofiest thing was, my head started flashing movies of Ricky to me. Like last night when he kept licking that spy guy, and wouldn't let him up. A couple a times it felt like a laugh was coming on me, I swear. Then I thought of my Dad, and how he was always after me to take care of my room. Darn, why would I think of that? My room was as good as a million miles away right then.

Then there was a movie in my head of me and Jimmy running away from the house. Even the house seemed like it was across the galaxy. It just hit me, like a television picture playing in my mind, my Dad calling after us. I'd never seen him so mad. There, right before my eyes, was a movie of him yelling at me. Mom too, and their voices pounded in my ears like they were really there. Right then, I wanted so bad for it to be true. Didn't care what the punishment was, I'd be glad to take it.

While all this was going on inside my skull, Jimmy started making noise from underneath the tape across his face. It took me a minute to come back to the basement from the trip I was taking in my brain. He was moaning pretty loud, and somehow that made me return to earth, but I still couldn't figure out what he wanted. Then he rolled a couple a times 'til he bumped into me. He kept shaking his body, and jolting me with his shoulders, and mumbling something. Only thing I could figure out is he wanted me to turn over. It was only a guess, but that guess was all I had to go on, so I did it. Then he bent

152

his knees, and dragged himself down to where my hands were tied behind my back. After he rubbed his face against my hands a couple a times, I knew he wanted me to pull off his tape. Not being able to see made it hard, but he kept shoving his face into my hands 'til I caught the edge of the tape. It started to rip away from his face kinda slow. Could tell by how hard it was coming off that it must have been hurting him a little.

"Good job," Jimmy said, "now roll over, and put your face near my hands."

The floor rubbed my skin a little, but it would be worth it just to have my mouth working again. As it worked out, Jimmy found my face easy enough, all of it. He played with my eyes, nose, and ears awhile before he got to my mouth. When he ripped the tape off, I almost went through the ceiling. It must've hurt Jimmy a lot more than I had thought.

"Owww," I started to cry out.

"Shut up," he stopped me.

"Are you crazy," I whispered. Our business had now switched from being in danger, to being in pain.

"It's better to do it fast!"

"Say's who?"

"Let's not argue about it now."

There was no real reason to argue, I knew fast or slow, the ripping off of the tape was gonna hurt and hurt bad; but when it was being ripped away from your face, somehow it just made you want to yell and complain about it. I figured that all out in my head, so I put the brakes on my big mouth, and stopped, and thought for a minute

153

about more important things. What I was thinking made me kinda sad, but it seemed like the truth, so I said it.

"Jimmy..."

"Yeah?"

"Man, I think we bought it."

He thought for a minute then said, "What is it James Bond always says when he's in trouble like this?"

"Come off it Jimmy, we ain't James Bond," I really didn't want to play any games right then.

"Come on, what's he say?"

"Jimmy."

"Shawn!"

"I don't know."

So, he was gonna tell me whether I wanted to play or not. "He always says we ain't dead yet."

"I don't remember him saying… How do ya' figure we ain't dead yet," remember I was still kinda mad at him for wishing us into this situation.

"It doesn't matter," he stopped me in my tracks. "That's the way we got to act if we want to get out of here alive. Trust me," he said again.

"Oh sure, you got us this far, right?"

"Look we're getting closer all the time. Remember, all we gotta do is get up the stairs to the box."

"You really flipped this time. These things are cuttin' our wrist and..."

"Keep it low," he warned me again.

"Nobody's gonna hear us, nobody will probably ever hear from us again."

"Stop feeling sorry for yourself!"

"Who else is gonna feel sorry for me?"

"Come on, we gotta get out of here."

"These things are cuttin' me bad, if I move... and I think my legs bleeding. Besides, that ink in my eyes is startin' to really burn!"

"Stop complaining!"

"Look the only way we're getting out of here, is if James Bond or Batman come in through that window right now, and tear them guys apart." He could tell how mad I was now, and I'm sure he knew how scared. "Go 'head, take your choice, 'cause none of 'em are gonna show!"

"What I'm saying is, we can't depend on anybody but ourselves, and if we're going to get out of here..."

"Come off it, we bought it! Those guys are probably out there digging a hole to toss us into right now."

"We have bought it, if you don't help me."

I thought real long and hard on it. It didn't seem like anything we did could hurt much, and if I could still help my parents and my sister, that would be great.

"Well, what do you say," he asked me again.

"Let's go Batman," I said.

"All right, Boy Wonder, let's go into action." He sounded excited as he started to look around. "How many times have we been down here with the Professor?"

"Once... twice," I answered, not sure why he was asking. "Why?"

"Because we've gotta use our heads if we're gonna get out of here."

"Like how," I was putting more trust in Jimmy's head, than in mine.

"Lucky for us these things are made of plastic, and not handcuffs."

"But we can't move."

"Sure we can, we just did."

"All we did was roll."

"That'll get us part of the way there. The rest of the way we'll have to help each other."

"These plastic cuffs are cuttin' me bad."

"We already talked about that," he said like he was just gonna forget about the hurtin', so I might as well do the same. "Now we got to do it!" There was no use questioning things. Wasn't sure I wanted to. "What do you keep in basements," he said.

Thought about it for a second, "Junk ya' don't wanna keep upstairs."

"What kinda junk?"

"Old junk, I guess."

"Like..." he said, and kept me hanging.

"Jimmy, if you know the answer, don't keep me guessin'."

"Just thinking, I'm sure I saw some old tools down here. Wrenches, hammers, that sort of stuff."

"How's that gonna help?'

"Maybe there's a pair of old wire cutters lying around."

"They'd have to be over in that metal closet." Saw that looking over his shoulder. The little bit of sunlight coming into the basement mixed with the shaky memories of the place. It was almost hidden in the shadows, but I could still make it out standing against the far wall.

"That s a good start," he said.

"Even if we get over there, how we gonna stand up, and open it?"

"First let's get over there, then we'll think of what to do next."

Sounded like the best idea all day. Only problem, every time I rolled the floor rubbed off more skin, and the plastic ties cut deeper into my wrist and ankles. I'm sure that Jimmy was going through the same, but neither of us said another word. Just squirmed, and wiggled, and rolled our way across the basement. My legs must have been scraped pretty bad by the time we got there, not to mention my shoulders, chest, and whatever you could think of. All at once we heard some footsteps traveling across the ceiling, we both stopped, and held our breath, afraid that any second the door at the top of the stairs would open, and we'd be caught in the wrong place at the wrong time. Lucky break for us, the footsteps just kept moving along. When we got to the metal closet, we stopped.

"Now's the fun part," said Jimmy.

"What if it's locked," I wondered about that.

"Don't say that!"

"Just wonderin'..."

"Well don't!"

Jimmy thought on it for a minute, and then spoke to me again. "If I use your feet," he said, "to lean against, I think I can get to my knees if you push me up."

"Then what?"

"Wait 'til we get there."

So, he lied flat, swung his legs up and down, and then threw his head up in the air, bringing his shoulders up with it. Jimmy was able to use his arms a little to push up, but not too much. Next thing I knew he's pushing himself against my feet.

"Owww, that hurt," 'cause when he fell back on me he landed kinda hard.

"It didn't feel so good to me either," he came back.

"Now you're gonna have to push hard with your legs to get me up."

"Huh?"

"Use your knees, bring 'em into your body."

"I already scratched my back up pretty good just getting here."

"What do you think those guys are planin' to do to us?"

"I'll do it, I'll do it," I said quick like, 'cause Jimmy had a good point.

Didn't like it, but I did it anyway. All I could feel was my shoulders and back scraping against that cold cement floor; and was wondering if I'd have any skin worth saving by the time this was all over. That move seemed to help a little. Jimmy threw his head forward, and was now on his knees.

"So far, so good," he said.

"What now?"

"Now, I gotta try and reach the handle." Jimmy tried hard to pick his arms up behind his back high enough, but just missed grabbing the handle. "Darn," he said.

"What's a matter?"

"Just can't make it."

"Told ya' it was a waste of..."

"Shut up, and help me get to my feet." He sounded mad that time. Strange, how we were keeping our voices low, but at the same time yelling at each other.

"What do ya' want me to do?"

"Let's see," he stopped to think again.

"This is killin' me." Remember I was still rolled onto my back, and it was grinding into the cold cement.

"Shut up. Got it! Get tighter to the closet. Put your head on the door, and see if you can push off with your back, and sit up."

"With my head?"

"Gotta better way?"

"Why didn't ya' think of this when you were getting up?"

"Come on, come on," he rushed me. There were a couple clangs as my head hit the cabinet. "Shhh," said Jimmy.

"What am I supposed to do?"

"Don't worry about your head Shawn. Try and push up with your arms a little." I moaned trying not to think of the pain. "Keep it down!" Jimmy was making almost as much noise as me with his quiet yelling.

Being tied, my arms weren't much help, but they got me up a little. "What am I supposed to do?"

"Take it slower."

Finally, after smashing the back of my head into the door three or four times, and almost falling onto my face, I was able to get to my knees. Every time my head smacked into the door, I got a quick "Shhh" from Jimmy, like he thought I liked banging my head into metal doors. When I finally got up, I had to keep my head pressed against the cabinet door, so that I wouldn't fall.

"Good, good," said Jimmy.

"Good for you!"

"Now just don't move. I gotta use you to get to my feet."

"What are ya' gonna do?"

"Prop myself against you for support. Try and bounce my way up. Stay close to the cabinet, so you can catch me if I start to fall"

"We could both… How am I gonna catch you?"

"Don't move!" He wasn't listening to me. Where was I going? Jimmy dug his chin into my shoulder.

"Ow," I let go with another cry.

"Shut up!"

Then he pushed off of me, and made his way onto his feet. For a second he rocked back and forth, and bounced a little trying to catch his balance. You could swear he was gonna topple over. Then he stopped moving, and stood there straight up. He stood there, and held his breath, like he wasn't sure he was gonna be able to stay standing for too long.

"Why didn't you use the cabinet instead of me?"

"Yeah, I probably should have, but I wanted to use you for support."

"What!"

"If I landed on you I wouldn't make as much noise that I would if I hit the floor or the cabinet."

"Are you crazy?"

With his plan we'd both fall, me getting the worst of it for being on the bottom. Yeah, Jimmy was planning to use old Shawn for a cushion.

"Edge your way back a little," Jimmy said, he just wasn't listening.

"How am I gonna do that?" He was telling me to do stuff that I'd have to be a circus acrobat to do.

"Well don't then!"

After he said that, Jimmy started hopping back to the handle of the cabinet. When he got there, he almost knocked me down.

"Watch it, will ya'!" Now I was not only afraid of the guys upstairs catching us, but that I was gonna crack my skull if Jimmy fell on me.

He didn't answer me; he just turned around, and tried to get hold of the handle. Stretching his arms backwards, Jimmy was now able to get his hands on it. Then he jerked the handle a couple of times, but nothing happened. It made some noise, too much noise. I cringed as I waited for somebody upstairs to hear it, and come running down the steps. We both stood still for a long minute, and prayed for nothing to happen. Then Jimmy turned back to me.

"It's locked," he said.

"You've gotta be kiddin' me."

There was now a little more sunlight coming in through the window, so we could see a little better.

"Hold on, there's a work table over here." He said it without hearing a word I had said.

"How you gonna get there, climb on my back, and let me carry ya'?"

"No, smart guy, I'll hop."

"If ya' fall your face is gonna get flattened on that cement."

"I'll just have to try not to fall then."

Jimmy didn't say another word. He just started hopping towards the worktable. A couple a times Jimmy stopped to catch hold of his balance. For a second he'd look like he was gonna go crashing to the floor, then he'd catch himself, and wobble until he was able to stand still, and start hopping all over again. When he reached the table, he called back in a low voice across the basement.

"Pay dirt!"

That was my signal to start crawling over that way. Got on my back. It seemed like miles of rough floor ahead as I wiggled, and rolled, and pushed with my feet to get to where Jimmy was. While I was trying to get to him, he was spinning around to get his back to face the table. When I had finally squirmed my way to where his feet were, I asked him what he had found.

"A small hatchet, the Professor must use it to chop firewood."

"Can ya' reach it?"

"Think I can... Got it!" He pulled and pulled, but he just couldn't seem to move it.

"What's a matter?"

"Just hard with these things on my wrist." After a second he said, "watch it, here it comes."

It came all right, he made a real hard pull, and the hatchet came flying off the table, and headed right to the floor and my head. Rolled out of the way quick like, and almost screamed when the blade just about missed crashing into my skull.

"Ahhh," I started to cry out but, before Jimmy could say anything, I said it for him. "Shut up, I know... What are ya' trying to do, kill me?"

"Sorry, that was an accident."

Didn't want to talk about it, just wanted to get out of there. Since my head wasn't split open, the near hatchet to the head was something that I could always yell about later. We stayed real quiet for a minute, scared that some of the men upstairs might have heard the hatchet hitting the floor. Luckily, the wooden handle had hit first with a thud, and the metal blade just dropped a small way.

Jimmy slid down to the floor, sliding his back against the edge of the worktable. Then he helped me sit up, so that we were back to back. He gave me the hatchet to hold in between my hands, and started rubbing the plastic tie that was wrapped around his wrist against the blade. Told him it'd probably hurt, but Jimmy didn't care. Heard him give out with little cries every time the blade would accidentally cut into him, or it tugged too hard on the plastic. In a few minutes Jimmy's hands were free. Then it was my turn.

He surprised me. Since he now could see what he was doing, he made it easy on me. Put my hands to the floor, and sawed through the plastic, didn't hurt a bit that way. The feet were no problem. Now both of us were up and ready. Ready for what I really didn't know. Guess for whatever was in Jimmy's crazy head. After all he had gotten us this far.

CHAPTER 11. THE GREAT ESCAPE

Boy was I wrong. Thought that the first time up in the sky with the Gravity Box was the scariest thing that had ever happened to me. Nope, that was looking kinda weak next to all the other crazy stuff that had gone on the night before and this day. Now we were going up those basement stairs. Turned out that what seemed to be the scariest thing ever was changing every five minutes. 'Cause if those guys in black were up there, and caught us again, we were really dog meat, and they wouldn't be waiting to feed us to the dogs.

We were at the point of no return. That's what Jimmy said. What that meant was, that it was just as crazy to try and run away, as it was to go ahead with his plan to save the Professor, and steal the other Gravity Box. Now we could've really used James Bond, and I wished he had taken on this assignment instead of us.

We we're trying to walk as softly as we could, but every step was creaking, and making noise for us. No matter how hard we tried, the old steps wouldn't cooperate, so we took them as slow as possible, and hoped that if anybody heard us, they would just think it was the house settling. That's what my Mom always told me it was, when those scary noises came creeping out from the basement at home. Any second we were waiting for the door to swing open, and we'd get nabbed. The scariest part was when we finally made it to the top step, and had to open that door. The only thing we could both think of was the last time we had turned that handle from the other side. I don't think either of us could breathe 'til we could peek out. Nothing happened, and that was the best thing that could have happened. With Jimmy's head sticking out and around the door, he couldn't see none of the guys in black. Waiting wasn't gonna get us anywhere. Whatever they had planned for us, they had to come back to do it. No use us being there when they did. Our best chance was away from the basement, and into the lab. Jimmy said that to go back to the woods would be crazy, 'cause they'd still have some men out there keeping an eye out for unwelcome visitors. Sounded good to me, either way I was scared out of my head. The first place we went to was the living room. That was the fastest way to the lab. Since we didn't hear any voices coming from there, we edged along the wall. Actually I did, and Jimmy told me not to. He said that the grease marks would give them a trail, so I stopped doing it. Later, if I was still alive, I could always help the Professor clean up the mess. I was really hoping for a later on, and all the housework that went along with it. The room was empty with nobody around, and the hallway that led to the lab was opened wide. On the table were Jimmy's briefcase and the darts.

"This is too good to be true," Jimmy whispered.

"You think this is good?"

"They've given us our chance back."

Me, well I just shook my head, and picked up my darts. In my mind it didn't seem like all that much of a chance we were getting back. Mainly since this junk didn't work most of the time. We had a rolling briefcase, and a couple of firecrackers, and some other junk to use against those guys, and whatever super weapons they probably

166

had. Oh, and guns too, didn't want to forget about the guns. There was also a chance that they found the other Gravity Box, and if that happened, it was all over for sure.

"Do ya' think they left yet," I said real quiet like; we were still in our whisper mode. The idea just hit me, 'cause we didn't see or hear anybody.

"No, why would they just leave us?"

"Maybe they thought we'd just rot down there, somethin' like that."

"Don't think so, these guys are too thorough for that."

"Darn, I hate it when you make so much sense."

"There's no more time for talk, now we gotta act." Nothing Jimmy could say was making me happy today.

Before I knew it, Jimmy went through the hallway, briefcase in one hand, exploding dart in the other ready to fire. I followed. Halfway down the hallway that connected the lab and the house we began to hear voices again. At first, we couldn't make out what they were talking about, but it sounded like that big, blonde guy's voice. That slowed us up a little. There was a door at the other end of the hall, and that opened into the lab. On the other side we hoped would be the Gravity Box, and that we could get our hands on it; but for sure those other guys were there. Jimmy turned to me; he was dead serious and scared to death. Could hear that in his voice, and see that in his eyes.

"We got one chance," he whispered.

"What's that?"

"One chance to get to the box. And they'll kill us to keep us from getting to it."

"Wish you didn't say that."

"You know it's true."

"I just didn't want to hear it." I shook my head sadly. "Want to wait," waiting seemed like a great idea to me.

"What for?"

"Maybe..."

"Keep it down, if we can hear them, maybe they can hear us." That shut me up super quick. "The only thing we got going for us is surprise. They don't know we're up here."

"But they wouldn't be worried about it either, would they?"

Jimmy held up the briefcase. "Got enough smoke bombs and fireworks left in here to create a few more great big diversions."

"Then what?"

"When they're looking the other way, we go for the machine."

"Aww man..."

"What else we got, what choices? It's like that guy said, if we run, it'll only take a little longer for them to hunt us down".

It took a minute, 'cause I was so scared out of my head, but I said it, "Go for it!"

Real quick like Jimmy poured some of the powder that was in a tin container in the case, and spread it all around the top of the case.

"What are ya' doing that for?"

"Makin' more smoke, come on help!" So, I did.

Any second we were waiting for somebody to come charging through that door. When Jimmy was done spreading the dark powder out, he attached the wheels to the bottom of the briefcase.

"What's that for?"

"Giving them a moving target." Then he handed me one of the dye-filled water pistols.

"What am I gonna do with this?"

"If worst comes to worst, shoot them."

"You do know its only dye?"

"It's our last and only chance. What do we got to lose?"

My fingers squeezed the trigger, and squirted the gun couple of times against the ceiling. Guess I did have nothing to lose, and some how that was the only thing that made me able to go on. I could have turned back, but to what? My parents and sister were in danger, death was all around me; so at a time like that charging right into the middle of a sure disaster seemed like an all right place to go.

"Ready," Jimmy whispered, pulling the lighter from out of its holder inside of the case. Didn't answer with my voice, don't think I could remember how to speak. Just bobbed my head up and down a couple a times to let him know that I was ready for whatever was gonna happen when we went through that door. On our tiptoes we walked to the door. Before we did anything, we stopped to listen a minute to what was happening on the other side. The first voice we could make out was the Professor, and he didn't sound happy.

"The world is not ready for my invention. I was a fool," said the Professor.

"Ready or not your gravity device is coming with us," that sounded like the spy boss, that blonde haired guy. Couldn't be sure it was him though.

"It is wrong," the Professor sounded like he was gonna cry. "It is all wrong. I will never cooperate!"

"I'm afraid you really don't have much choice Professor Burkhardt. You see you will be coming along with us also. And once you are back at our headquarters, I feel certain that you will have a change of heart."

"But that is kidnapping!"

"Get some of the Professor's clothes," the voice was ordering one of the other men.

"What will happen to those boys?"

"We're going to take good care of them," and the way he said it didn't sound like they were planning on sending us to Disney World.

There was no time to waste now, 'cause those guys must've been coming into the house to get the Professor's clothes. Had to go through the hallway for that, and to take "good care" of us. There was no choice now we had to do something. The whole plan was to just get our hands on the old Gravity Box. With that maybe we had a chance to stop those guys. That was if they didn't shoot us, or use the Gravity Box in the lab first, and if the first box was still in the closet. That was a ton of ifs, but like Jimmy said, what choice did we have. We could hear somebody's footsteps moving at us from behind the door.

"Ready," Jimmy asked.

"Ready," there was no place else to go.

Quick like he ducked down, and flicked the lighter. The darn thing misfired again, but a second shot sent the flame out, and lit the fuse that was lying in all the black powder on top of the briefcase. It was burning fast, but I wasn't sure it was fast enough. Meanwhile Jimmy lit up three of the smoke bombs at once. Like a last-minute thing, I pushed the water pistol down into my pants, and took out a couple darts. Didn't trust that stupid water pistol right then. This job called for heavy artillery.

The time was here whether we wanted it to be or not. The handle on the door had started to turn. Don't know what came over me next, but the idea just popped in my head out of nowhere. As Jimmy was getting ready to push the smoking briefcase, which by the way wasn't smoking yet, out into the lab, I decided to kick the door open real hard. Must've really caught the guy behind it by surprise, 'cause it knocked him back, and almost sent him flying across the worktable.

Right then, all eyes were on us. A great bunch of gray smoke puffed up off of the rolling briefcase just in the nick of time.

"What the..." I heard the spy boss start to yell.

Besides the Professor and the spy boss there were two other guys dressed in black standing in that room. Jimmy was quick to drop the other smoke bombs in front of us, and shove the briefcase across the floor. Now we couldn't see them, but we had to hope they couldn't see us either. What we wanted them to do was think we were behind the briefcase, and go after that.

"Don't hurt those boys," I heard the Professor yell out.

171

"Get them," the spy boss ordered his men. He didn't sound like he cared if we got hurt or not.

As we stepped through the cloud of smoke, everybody including the Professor was watching the rolling smoke coaster that Jimmy had sent in the direction away from us.

Still on our tiptoes we ran to the closet. It was Jimmy this time, and not me who made the mistake, by banging into the table that was filled with trays of test tubes. When they went crashing to the ground everybody knew where we really were. That boss guy was the first one to see us. While the others were busy trying to grab hold of arms full of smoke, the guy in charge started after us.

"Over here, you fools," he called to his men, who right away let go of the empty air they were trying to get hold of.

That big blond guy was gonna get to us first, and boy did he look mad. Even the Professor was helping out. When he saw what was coming down, he put his foot out, and tripped the spy boss, who crashed right to the floor.

That gave us a few more seconds, but the closet was still a few feet away, and so were those two other men in black, who were coming our way fast. Even the boss guy was up on his feet quick, and after us in no time flat. Without even thinking about it, my hand tossed the dart hard at the floor in front of the two guys in black. The explosion shook them a little, 'cause they dropped back. Jimmy threw another dart in front of the spy boss. It was a pretty good explosion too, and made him stop, but just for a second. The darts weren't all that dangerous, but they looked and sounded like they could be. We were getting close to the closet, but all too soon everybody was right

172

after us again. So, at the top of my lungs, I screamed at them as I raised the other dart over my head.

"Stand back you creeps, or this one's got your name on it!'

That sounded cheesy I know, but it stopped the two guys in black, but the blond one wouldn't listen. He kept charging at us. I cocked my arm back, and he didn't even flinch, he just kept coming.

"Leave the boys alone," the Professor was playing that song again, but nobody seemed to be listening.

Couldn't really throw the dart right at the guy, so this one blew up close to his feet too. It didn't stop him, not for a second.

"They're just kids," the head guy called to the other two. And he was just about ready to grab me, when Jimmy quick like drew out his own water pistol, and squirted him right in the face. That fast the hands went to cover his face, and he started yelling about his eyes burning.

The other two must've thought this was their chance, and rushed right in to take us. Jimmy pulled out another dart. That made the guys in black divide, and start circling us. One started moving around the nearby desk. Didn't think Jimmy could hold them both off that way with one dart, so I pulled out my own water pistol, and started squirting it at him. The one I was aiming at put his hands up to block the dye, and kept turning his head.

We edged back a little, as the closet was real close now. If we waited any longer, they'd have us. Rushing to the closet, I swung the door open. As I did the outside door to the lab swung open too, and a bunch more of the guys in black came rushing in to the lab. Guess they heard all our noise from outside. They had to stop for a minute to

173

make sense of what was happening, and while they did that, I had to get my hands on the old Gravity Box.

"Get them," the spy boss screamed out again, still rubbing the dye from his eyes. There wasn't much light, but there it was lying right on the floor, underneath some old newspapers.

Jimmy took his other dart, and threw it at the new guys just coming in, and then he rushed into the closet, and closed the door behind him.

"You got it," he screamed.

"Did a second ago, before you made it all dark." We were screaming back and forth.

But I had a good idea where I'd seen it. So after a quick feel around on the floor, I had it. Jimmy was pulling on the door handle, but he wasn't strong enough to do any good.

"What now," I yelled.

There was one good tug at the door, and Jimmy almost went flying out of the closet, but at the last second he put his foot to the inside wall hard enough to close the door one more time. Really didn't think he was strong enough to do it, but somehow, he did. Guess when you're scared enough you get a lot stronger.

"Get hold of the handles," he yelled back to me.

That only took a second.

"Got 'em," I yelled.

Jimmy didn't wait any longer; he let go of the doorknob, and ran back next to me. The door swung open wide, and a couple of the men in black were standing in front of the bright light coming into the closet.

"Jimmy," I wanted an answer, to be told what to do.

"Make a picture of these guys flying away!"

Closed my eyes real fast. Couldn't see any picture at first.

"Blast 'em," Jimmy screamed out.

Then I saw it, they were flying away from us, shooting through the air, soaring to the clouds. Opened my eyes to see if it had happened. It hadn't.

"Think harder," Jimmy yelled. The men were now in the closet. One bent over, and started to grab Jimmy. He was the closest.

Squeezed my eyes shut tight this time, and held my breath. The second guy in had now reached me, and was pulling me up. I struggled not to let go of the box. The picture was better now. The handlebars tingled in my hands. He pulled hard again, and then suddenly let go of me. When I peeked through my eyelids, the green beam had shot out of the front of the box. The man it hit screamed, and a second later he bounced off of the ceiling. The other man in black jumped back and around the wall, but that didn't help him none. The beam chased him, and curved right around the outside of the closet. He screamed too when the wave of green light threw him against the wall, and continued to toss him upwards smacking him into the ceiling.

"Get in there," that was the guy with the blond hair yelling again, and he was sure doing a lot of that that day.

Guess he had gotten the ink out of his eyes by now. The men in black weren't being quiet anymore. All the others were stomping across the floor to get to us.

"Think... think," Jimmy yelled at me.

Closed my eyes real tight again. The box started shaking, worse than ever. Guess it knew how scared I was. Without me wanting it to, it started to pull me out of the closet. Maybe I did kinda picture myself away from that place, maybe a little. Whatever the reason, it was starting to pick my legs up into the air.

"What are you doing," Jimmy couldn't figure out what was happening either. Just then two more of the bad guys showed up at the door. Like without me telling it, the Gravity Box knew what to do all by itself, it shot a blast of green light right into them, and then they shot to the top of the lab. Could hear a couple a thuds when they crashed against the ceiling, and seemed to bounce off of it a couple times. There were some cries from the pain, but I don't think any of them were hurt too bad, mostly scared.

When Jimmy saw my feet floating in the air, he ran over to me, and grabbed me like he was trying to pull me down.

"What are you doing," he yelled again, but the other guy at the door stopped me from answering.

"What the…" I started to say to myself, "he's got a gun!"

"Hold it right there," he ordered us, but the machine still having a mind of its own, blasted him through the closet door. The sound of a gun firing rang out, but the green beam had just tossed him and the bullet upwards, and away from us. Now another one of them was decorating the ceiling. It looked so strange the way they were all stuck up there, and a couple of them were even trying to crawl their way back to the floor. But the power of the beam seemed to keep them glued like mice on a trap. When Jimmy grabbed hold of me, it was like electricity shooting through the both of us, and his legs started floating too.

"What are you," he tried to ask me one more time, but the Gravity Box didn't seem like it wanted to listen, and had a whole different idea. Maybe it was my idea, it could've been, I guess. Like a rocket we zoomed out of the closet, almost knocking over the one guy left to come after us. The guy in charge, he ducked to the floor just in time before we crashed into him. Both me and Jimmy started to yell as the box and us headed towards the window. The boss guy was pulling out his own gun, when all around us the other guys in black began to crash to the floor, 'cause the green beam was no longer making them float up. One guy dropped onto the spy boss, and knocked the gun from his hand. A couple of them fell down, and broke some pretty expensive lab stuff. Another one hit a weak spot in the floor, and almost went through it. Caught a quick glimpse of his head and chest sticking out of the floor. We were just about to smack into the window, when another green blast shot out of the box, and sent the glass and wood up into the air, and out of our way. As we soared through the place where the window once was, I couldn't believe my eyes. I know that Jimmy couldn't either. The broken glass fell like raindrops around us, but never touched us. A second later the box and us were soaring up into the sky.

"What are you doing," this time Jimmy got the question out, and I had time to answer.

"This is what my head wanted to do, I guess."

"But this wasn't the plan!"

Plan or not, the only picture I could get in my head was of us getting out of the lab, and that's what the box had done. We must've already been a hundred feet high, when something whistled past my ear. Didn't look to see, but it felt like somebody had shot at us, and there was probably more bullets headed our way.

CHAPTER 12. STALKING THE STALKERS

Guess it was the idea of getting shot that made me, the box, and Jimmy fly over the trees, so that we couldn't see the lab, and nobody at the lab could see us. I was so scared, and flying so fast, for a second I was afraid that Jimmy was gonna let go. Jimmy felt light, like he wasn't even there. Must've been the box doing that too. As we headed away from the lab and into town, Jimmy asked me one more time what was I doing.

"Gotta get back to my place, those guys still got my Mom, and Dad, and sister." Guess I was being selfish, but that's the way I felt about it, now that I had a way to save them. I wasn't thinking about the Professor, nothing like that, just my family.

"Can't do that," Jimmy called out, and he had to do it kinda loud, 'cause we were whizzing over the treetops real fast now.

"Why not?"

"Gotta get the Professor first."

"That's easy for you to say, your parents are back home, and all right."

Didn't really believe it was easy for Jimmy, but right then it was the only thing I could think to say.

"You know better than that," he yelled so I could hear him, and acting mad like I had said it at all, and I knew I shouldn't have put it that way, but all I could think about was my family.

"But I gotta do somethin'!"

"We're gonna do it!"

"What!"

It was hard for us to talk shouting over the wind, so Jimmy told me to slow down a little, and to listen to his plan.

"First thing you gotta know is that whoever got these machines has the whole ball of wax."

"Huh?"

"The country whose got this machine, doesn't have to worry about missiles, doesn't have to worry about lasers, or anything like that. The ones who got hold of this baby will be in charge of it all!"

"Ya' mean..."

"They'll rule the world. They could sink anybody else's ships, or down their planes."

"Geez, never thought of that!"

"So, they gotta get hold of us, they're not gonna want another one of these machines hanging around. That would make whoever has it equal."

"Then..."

"We gotta stop them first."

"But my Mom and…"

"They probably won't hurt them. They'll need them to bargain with. First they've gotta talk to us."

"So?"

"So, they'll expect us to go to your house. We can't do anything we're expected to do. If they can't get hold of us they can't bargain with us."

"Then what?"

"We don't let them get set up, we attack!"

"How?"

"Come on, let's really test out the Gravity Box"

"But don't they got one too?"

"Let's hope they don't know how to use it yet."

"Yeah, let's hope!"

"Ready?"

"They got bullets."

"Don't sweat it."

Who was he kidding? We were both sweating it. Actually, our first plan was to save the Professor, but we never decided how we were gonna do that. As we circled high above the trees in the forest, and headed back to the lab, which I really didn't believe we were going back to, we had to think of something.

"Why don't I just make a picture in my head them all floating away," I said.

"It's a start," Jimmy said.

When I looked back to see him still holding onto me, I could see he was into some serious thinking. That tipped me off that he wasn't too happy with my idea, but just said that he was, so that he could keep me happy while he thought of something better. Didn't think it was such a bad plan though. A second later I made a picture in my head of the box stopping right in the sky.

"What are you stopping for," Jimmy stopped his thinking, so he could yell at me some more.

"'Cause the labs right behind those trees... what do ya' wanna do?"

There was like a second in his eyes where I could tell he was still working on that plan, and then that quick he had it. His eyes lit up, they told the whole story.

"Got it!

"Well?"

"We just don't make those guys float away. We make the whole house do it."

"What's that gonna do?"

"With the lab, and everything in it shooting up into the sky, they won't have time to go for their guns. They'll be too busy dodging tables, and test tubes, and the room, and stuff."

"Do ya' think it'll work?"

"No sweat!" There were those words again. "Now what ya' gotta do," he said, "is just don't picture the whole lab coming up at once. First you make them start flying."

"While they're still inside?"

"Why not?"

"Sounds good," I said, and it did.

"What about the guys stationed outside?"

"After you tear the roof off of the place, and everyone starts pouring into the sky, they ain't gonna shoot us, 'cause they'll be afraid we're gonna drop everyone else."

"Ya' think," 'cause I wasn't sure.

"I'm guessing that's what they'll do."

Glad he didn't say no sweat. The lab was just beyond the trees, and we made it there fast. Down below, it didn't look like anybody was around.

"Ready," I asked Jimmy.

"Remember, one piece at a time, but fast so they got no time to think."

"I know, I know!"

Just then my eyes closed, and the picture was starting to appear in my head, but before it could be seen real easy, Jimmy stopped me.

"Shawn!"

"What?"

"Open your eyes, and look down."

So, I did. What was down there didn't make me happy. The spy boss had just stepped out onto the porch with the new Gravity Box. Behind him were some of the other guys in black and the Professor. The spy boss spotted us instantly. He didn't call out, or try to warn us. Just pointed the front of the new gravity machine at us like it was a canon. Like in no time a green burst of light shot out of the hole in the front of the other box, and was headed right at us. It didn't give us anytime to think about it, it just came zooming our way. It was like a split second before it hit us when our box zoomed us sideways, so that the green beam missed zapping us. Missed us by inches.

"Good work," Jimmy said to me, but I hadn't done anything, not that I could think of.

"Let's get the heck out of here!"

But that idea had come too late, another green blast was on its way. This time I could see the picture in my head. It was of us flying behind a tree that just caught my eye. The box and us shot across the sky, and circled around the tree, almost flinging Jimmy off of me.

"What are you doing you crazy..." he started to say, but then he caught sight of the green beam that had just missed us traveling off into space.

"Good work," he said again. "Picture us out of here!"

That idea was just as good the second time around. Now the box was acting even before the pictures could be seen in my mind, like it was a bodyguard looking out for us. Another beam blasted out of the Gravity Box below, and cut through the sky as we darted off. Just as we had gotten out of the way, the green light crashed against a tree that had been behind us. It was almost like lightening striking. As if by magic, the whole tree glowed with a bright green light. From over a giant pine, we could see the big tree start to tremble, and then fall. The gravity of the tree had become too strong for its own roots.

"This guy means business," I said.

"Go! Go," Jimmy screamed in my ear.

Started to shift into high gear, but before they were out of sight, I saw the blond guy leap into the air holding onto the box.

"Aw no," I said. "What's your plan now? So far this one wasn't too good."

"You're so smart, you think of something."

I could tell by his voice he didn't care for my attitude, but because there was a guy that was trying to shoot us out of the sky, coming up quick in the rear, this was not the time to argue. There really didn't seem like there was too much time for arguing that day. I

184

wondered if the spy boss had a gun. Then I thought why worry about a gun, that was the least of our problems.

What I saw in my head was just us rocketing away from the danger, and that's exactly what we did. Like at super speed we shot across the sky. If felt like it'd be easy to lose the spy boss, but when Jimmy looked back, that guy was too close for comfort.

"Try and lose him will you," Jimmy hollered at me.

"Where we gonna do that?" That's what I said, 'cause all that was in front of us was clear, blue sky. Not a cloud to be seen. It was our dumb luck that the sky hadn't been this nice in years.

"Go down low, maybe behind some trees," Jimmy said.

"Got ya'!"

Like before, the box didn't seem to want to wait for the pictures. It was like it knew we were in trouble, and just wanted to help out. Like the Salt and Pepper ride at the amusement park, we nose-dived at the ground. Could feel Jimmy squeezing tighter around my hips, trying desperately not to fall off. Knew the feeling, 'cause my grip was harder on the handlebars then ever before.

We both let loose with a loud "WHOA," as we dropped from the sky like a dive-bomber. Once we got down lower, the box was doing a great job of zipping in and out of the trees. A couple of times we had some close calls, missing low hanging branches only by inches. There were a couple blast of green light shooting out of this bad guys box, and smashing into trees along the way. Our luck was holding, but trees weren't so lucky as they started toppling all around us. Don't know how I was doing it. Not really sure I was doing it, but it did remind me of some video games we would play. Only instead of playing with the controls, you only had to think out your moves.

"Slow down," Jimmy screamed. Think he was getting a little nervous.

"Where's that guy?"

When Jimmy looked back, he could see the spy boss closing in on us, and fast.

"Don't slow down, don't slow down," Jimmy yelled again.

Guess this spy boss guy played some video games himself. The only reason he hadn't caught up to us yet, was that he needed a little more practice with his Gravity Box, and he had to guess our moves, but he was learning fast, too, too fast.

"This ain't working," I called back to Jimmy.

"Don't think that way, the box is liable to think you want to give up. To stop."

"I'm too scared to see that picture!"

It didn't feel good down low, so I decided on my own to climb again.

"Hold on," I told Jimmy, which was really something I didn't need to remind him to do. He was squeezing me real tight now, making it hard to breathe.

In front of us was a big oak. Instead of going around it, I decided to climb straight up the front of it. It was a good move at the right time, 'cause the guy chasing us just missed zapping us with another green bolt of lightning from his own Gravity Box, hitting the tree right where we had been a second before. The tree began to glow green, as we flew straight up the front of it. Only the top of the tree must have grown heavy, too heavy for the bottom half, 'cause it cracked in the middle, and started to fall. Like a missile it began to torpedo right at us. The box swerved us out of the way, just before the tree could crush us.

"Timber," I yelled as we sped on by it.

"That guys killin' all the trees," Jimmy called back to me.

"Creep!"

All that was in front of me, as we flew straight on up, was a clear blue sky. We had reached the far end of town, just on the outskirts. Below that there was still nothing but trees. Then just ahead we saw them, giant clouds hanging out over the edge of the city. They seemed like they were just there waiting for us. A big one right in front of us looked so white, 'cause it was surrounded by the bluest sky I'd ever seen. A plan came to me quick and fast. Not only was it a great idea, but it might top any that Jimmy would come up with all day.

"Swerve around a little," Jimmy hollered, "he might fire at us again."

"Good idea," I said, and then we started weaving back and forth, so the spy boss wouldn't know which way we were headed. Because Jimmy had broken my thought, I had a little trouble remembering my great plan. That always made me mad when that happened. Right when you were just about to be brilliant, you forget the best idea you ever had. Smart, huh? But as we kept climbing, the cloud hit my eye again, and like a shot, the thought came racing back into my head. I looked back at Jimmy, and could see the spy boss closing in on us. Closer than he had ever been.

"Keep your eye on the road," Jimmy yelled at me.

"The cloud game," I yelled back to him.

"Huh," he didn't know what I meant.

"The cloud game," I screamed as loud as I could. Without waiting for him to answer me, I took us right into the center of the big white cloud, and then he knew right away what I had in mind.

"Good idea," he yelled back. I'm sure he meant to say great idea.

"Keep quiet, we're gonna do some cloud hoppin'."

In just seconds we had disappeared from plain sight.

CHAPTER 13. THE CLOUD GAME

I'd hoped that the spy boss would have followed us right into that big cloud. That would've given us a good break, and a chance to beat this guy. I mean why were we doing all the running? We were better with the Gravity Box than he was. Maybe, 'cause running from bad guy spies sounded like the smart thing to do. But inside that cloud, if my plan worked, we just might bag us a bad guy. For like the longest time we waited. It was my guess, he was circling around that cloud, but since the Gravity Box didn't make any noise, how were we gonna know unless we bumped into him. And that would be a real bad way to find out where he was.

"Should we take a look out," I asked Jimmy in a whisper.

"What do you think," he whispered back.

Usually Jimmy didn't ask me what we should be doing about anything, so that threw me. For me hanging around and waiting, has always been the roughest thing to do. Like when you get into trouble and your Mom says, "wait until your father gets home." It was usually worst waiting for him to come home, than when he finally got there. Not always, but usually. So anyway, I decided to take a peek out. The Gravity Box started to move slowly around the cloud once again.

"Slow... slow," Jimmy whispered.

My head was barely through the side of the cloud, when I was glad I'd taken my time. The spy boss was still way down below, and rather than chase us into the clouds, he had made up his own plan. Using the Gravity Box, he had decided to turn the trees into missiles. After a quick burst of the green beam, the trees would lose their gravity, struggle to uproot, and then shoot off into the air, flying right through the clouds, right near where we would've been.

At first it was just one and two, then there were more, lots more. Twenty, thirty trees came flying right up at us, as if they were rockets launched from a launching pad.

We were just missed by a big one, when Jimmy said: "That creeps ruining the whole forest!"

"Could we worry about that later, right now we're gettin' torpedoed up here. Let's get out of here!"

"No," Jimmy said. I think he was taking charge again.

"Put the trees back where they belong!"

"But..." that's all I could think to say.

"That'll force him up here, and that's where we're good."

"Yeah, but..."

"That's what we want, right?"

"Right!"

Then the picture in my head saw the trees back in the ground. Just in time too, 'cause there was another one of them headed right at us. When the beam blasted out and struck the first tree, it somersaulted about three times, before starting to drop back into the ground. Guess now that tree didn't know which direction to head. Must've scared the heck out of blondie, 'cause all at once we could see the box and him zooming our way. That's when I decided to pop back into the cloud.

It was really misty in there as that cloud moved slowly on by us. We couldn't see him now, but I don't think he could see us either. In fact, I was sure of it. For a real long time, me and Jimmy kept as quiet as we could, hoping he wouldn't hear us. Then Jimmy had a thought, it wasn't exactly what either of us wanted to think about, but he said it anyway.

"What if he gets the same idea," he whispered.

"Huh?'

"What if he gets the same idea about weighing the cloud down with the both us in it?"

"Aww, man, whaddya have to think of that for?"

He just shrugged his shoulders as best as he could while hanging onto me.

The spy boss just might spray the whole cloud with the green beam. After all I'd thought of it myself. Thinking about that made it just too scary to hang around, so the picture I put in my head was of us rocketing over to the cloud next door. We moved so fast that even I was jolted. Jimmy almost got thrown off again. When we reached the other cloud, he let me have it for like the millionth time that day.

"Will you let me know when you're gonna do something like that!"

"Sorry."

"Well just watch it, I need the machine as much as you do to fly."

"Well, do you want to take the controls?"

"No," he said, and that surprised me. "You're the best one at this kinda' stuff."

"Gee, thanks!" We didn't usually say nice stuff to each other.

"Don't get all sappy on me. Right now we gotta be as smart as we can, and the smart thing to do is to let you do the driving."

"Thanks," I said again.

"Now, let's stick our heads out, and you blast that other cloud."

"Let's hope he's not waitin' for us."

"Nah, he's gotta be inside the cloud, he's gotta be."

Now Jimmy was hoping that that was true, and he wasn't the only one. Real slow like, we pulled ourselves up, and out of the mist. With our heads sticking out of the cloud, we could see nothing around but other clouds.

"He's still in there," Jimmy said.

"Ya' think," I said.

"I'm betting my life on it." So, who wasn't betting their life on it?

"Just zap it," I asked him.

"The whole thing."

"What if the cloud conks somebody on the head?"

"Its a cloud, it ain't gonna hurt them... I don't think."

It took a second to start getting the picture in my head. Jimmy pushed me. "Go! Go!"

"All right, cut me a break," I told him.

The picture was starting to come of blasting the whole cloud, but I had taken too long, 'cause the spy boss was starting to stick his head up out of the cloud. In a second he'd see us. Closed my eyes one more time.

"Hurry, please", Jimmy begged.

That was one favor he didn't have to beg for.

"I'm tryin', I'm tryin'!"

When my eyes opened the guy was halfway out of the cloud, and still no green beam came shooting out of the front of the Gravity Box. He was pretty far away, but you could tell he saw us too. His eyes and the box turned pointing right in our direction.

"Darn," I said.

"Do it!" Jimmy begged again.

Suddenly the front of the spy's Gravity Box lit up, and a beam shot out of it. Just then, like a delayed reaction, our box did the same thing. In no time flat the two beams crashed in midair, and exploded turning the whole sky bright green. The explosion sent me and Jimmy sailing back into the cloud. Guess it did the same to the other guy, but we were too busy flying through space to notice.

"Hold on," I yelled to Jimmy, who seemed like he was losing his grip.

"Got 'cha, got 'cha," he yelled back, almost crushing my ribs with his arms. We were upside down now, only I swear, I didn't know it. Didn't feel any different than being right side up. When we tried to fly under the cloud, we ended up on top again. Outside of the cloud there was no spy in sight. He had disappeared a second time.

"He must've been blasted back into the cloud like us," Jimmy said.

He didn't have to say anything else, 'cause old Shawn knew exactly what to do. It was easy this time to see the whole cloud turning green, and falling to the ground; and this time the machine listened to me the second the thought popped into my head. The beam must have been a half-mile wide. Like a giant water hose, the green blast sprayed out, and stretched across the whole width of the cloud. Now the whole thing glowed green, and started to plummet to the ground. Some of the white mist seemed to be fighting to stay up, but most of it was going down, and fast. As it fell, the cloud started to break up into pieces, and in between some of the pieces the man dressed in black was falling, falling and screaming. In his hands he no longer held onto the first Gravity Box. He looked like he was falling faster than the cloud, because I guess he weighed more than it did.

"Better stop him," Jimmy yelled at me.

I aimed the box, and it shot out like a giant green hand lifting him back into the air. The other box was still falling, and as the cloud broke up more, we could see the other box getting ready to crash down. That second Gravity Box was something that we really wanted, mostly me, 'cause Jimmy was beginning to wear a hole in my side. A second beam tossed the box back up into the air, and kept it up.

"Now we got two," I said.

"Get me over to it."

The spy guy kept yelling something at us, as we cruised over to the second box. While Jimmy got his hands his own Gravity Box, I called back to the guy who had been chasing us.

"Can't hear ya'!"

The giant green beam seemed to be bouncing him up and down in the air like a juggling ball. That wasn't my idea; at least I don't think it was. Anyway, it made me happy watching it.

"We can make a deal," that's what it sounded like he said, while the green beam was tossing him up and down in midair.

Started to get closer, so that he could make some sense.

"Don't get too close," Jimmy yelled to me.

"Don't worry, don't worry, "I wasn't as dumb as Jimmy thought I was. When I got close enough, but still out of reach, the box stopped.

"Whad ya want," I called to him.

"How would you like to trade that flying machine there for one mother, and father, and a little girl?'

"They'd better be all right," I told him, "or I'll drop you right now!"

Now he could tell that I was serious, 'cause he started trying to calm me down.

"Now don't get excited kid, stay calm!"

"My family better be all right, that's all I'm sayin'!"

A second later Jimmy got there. He could tell that the guy had me all upset.

"What's a matter," he asked me.

"He wants to trade the boxes for my family. Jimmy could see I was ready to cry again. So, he talked real quiet like, and I listened.

"Give him the boxes, and we've got nothing, nothing to bargain with, and nothing to protect ourselves with."

"What are you boys talking about," the spy boss called to us.

"What we have here is too important," Jimmy went on. "They will not want anybody left around who knows about it."

"The boy's parent's are with my men," the spy boss shouted out loud.

"Jimmy," I looked real fast at him.

The guy was still bobbing in the air, and talking like he was the one who had us.

"Let me put it this way Shawn, once he doesn't have to bargain, do you think he will?"

"Listen boy..." the spy tried to say.

"Shut up," I told him.

"Right now," Jimmy went on, "we are the two most powerful kids on the earth, think about it. We can shoot down missiles, leap over tall buildings, and all that good stuff."

"Whatever he's telling you, won't protect your Mother and Father, that little girl," the spy boss was yelling across the sky.

Jimmy shouted back at him, "once you get the gravity machines, you're not gonna do anything for us."

"You are talking nonsense kid," that creep called back. They were calling to each other back and forth.

"Then why do you want it so bad," Jimmy put him in his place, and then he looked at me. "If we can do all these amazing things, who's in a better position to save your parents?"

"My men are professionals, you'll never..."

"We already have," Jimmy told him.

Then the craziest thing happened. The blonde guy pulled out a gun.

"I'm taking those boxes now," he said. Then he pointed the barrel right at me. For a second, both me and Jimmy froze.

"Go ahead, shoot him," Jimmy said.

"What," I jumped in, 'cause what he said surprised me as much as the spy guy. "Jimmy!"

"The second he shoots you; you stop thinking about him, he becomes mashed potatoes on the rocks down there", and he looked at the ground. We all did.

"How high would you estimate we are," he asked the spy. "One thousand, two thousand feet up? You'd better just drop the gun."

"What if I just shoot you," the man turned the gun on Jimmy.

The thought blasted through my mind as I said the words, "Try and shoot him from up there."

Just then the green beam blasted even brighter shooting out of the front of the Gravity Box, and threw that guy like a canon ball about another twenty to thirty stories up into the air. The scream of terror coming out of him was something that I was getting use to. And let me tell ya', he cried like a baby all the way up.

"See if he'll drop it now," Jimmy said, as we climbed up there with him.

"A fall from up here," I told that creep, "and they won't even be able to make out it was you when ya' hit the dirt."

"Dental records," Jimmy said.

"What," I answered.

"If his teeth are still in his mouth, they'll be able to check his dental records."

"How are his teeth still going to be in his mouth," I asked Jimmy.

The guy must've believed we were serious, 'cause the gun just slipped out of his hand, and fell to the ground.

"What are we gonna do with him," I turned to Jimmy.

The spy boss was still just floating in front of us, but who knew what to do with him? Jimmy knew. Below us, close by, was the biggest tree around.

"Put him on top of that tree, 'til we can come back for him."

That guy's eyes almost bugged out of his head when he saw what we were planning to do with him.

"You must be crazy. The top of that tree will never hold me!"

"That's the chance we're gonna have to take," Jimmy said.

The way I was feeling about this guy right then, it was a chance I knew I was willing to take. But the guy might have been right, 'cause the branches got pretty slim near the top.

"Look, let's talk..." now the spy boss really wanted to bargain, and he wasn't sounding so tough anymore.

"It does look kinda shaky, so just keep still, don't try and climb down, and you'll probably be alright. No bear's gonna come climbing up there for you," Jimmy told him. "I don't think they climb that high anyway," he turned, and winked at me.

"Take me back with you," the spy boss tried to tell us, "I'll tell my men..."

"Afraid not," Jimmy cut him short.

"Don't put me..." but that's all he got out, 'cause I put him down real light on one of the high branches.

"Please, don't do this," he was sort of begging now.

"Just don't try, and climb down, stay real still, you'll be all right," Jimmy told him again. "I think," Jimmy shrugged.

"Don't think they'd even find his teeth if he fell from there," I said to Jimmy, but the once tough spy boss heard me.

"You kids are crazy," he screamed out, now looking really terrified.

"And if my parents and little sister are all right, we'll be back for ya'," I just wanted him to know, that I might forget where I put him if they weren't.

"But..." he tried to say.

It was too late to listen; me and Jimmy were already soaring skywards.

"Think he'll be alright," Jimmy said.

"I don't know, it was your idea."

"Think he's too scared, to try anything stupid, he'll be all right."

"Even if he climbs down, it'll take him a couple of hours."

"That's all the time we need."

"For what?"

"You know what dummy! For the two most powerful kids on earth to save the Professor, and your Mom, and Dad, and even that bratty little sister of yours. Heck maybe even save the whole planet."

"The whole planet?"

"If we get a few extra minutes, that's what we should definitely do."

"I'm all ready for that," I said, and Jimmy smiled at me.

"Today we are kinda' like Superman," Jimmy said.

"Kinda'," I said, and smiled back, 'cause I knew what he meant.

The higher we flew, the more like the Man of Steel I felt, and if you were Superman, who needed James Bond.

CHAPTER 14. THE MAN OF STEEL AT THE O.K. CORRAL

We were the Earp's, and the spies were the Clanton gang. The Earp's were the good guys, and the Clanton's were the bad guys in the days of the old west. The good guys against the bad guys, and we were headed towards the last round up. Gee, I love cowboy talk. Really from up there, where we were, it looked more like Superman versus the Clanton's. Either way, it was gonna be bad news for the spies. That's the way I was trying to think about it anyway, except all that was in my head, were the guns those other guys had. But Jimmy said not to worry about that, 'cause we were the two most powerful kids on the planet, maybe on any planet. Who knew for sure? Anyway, being the baddest dudes on one planet was plenty good enough for me.

There was still so much we didn't know yet. Like who were those guys in black, foreign agents? Who knew? How do you tell? I'd seen enough spy movies to know, that you could sound just like me, and still be a foreign agent. In fact, it was even better that way. Yeah, there were a lot of questions bouncing around inside my noodle. For instance, was my family okay? That was the main question pounding against the walls inside my head. If anything happened to them, those guys were gonna take a ride they'd never forget. Was really hoping that the Professor was all right too. There were all kinds of plans in my brain for those guys, if they had hurt anyone in my family, and at the same time, I didn't want anything bad to have happened, not to anybody. So that question was put out of my head, so I could think about Jimmy's plans. Of course, there was the problem of me flying this old Gravity Box, and I wanted to know if the Professor had time to get it fixed, before he got nabbed by the boys in black. Couldn't really worry about that now, just hoped it didn't throw me into outer space for another trip to the moon. So far, the box hadn't acted up, so I felt kinda confident with it.

From two different angles, we were gonna blast the house piece by piece into the sky. Thinking once way up in the sky, nobody would want to shoot us. They'd be afraid that we'd drop them on their heads. Good plan, huh?

Soon the lab was right ahead of us, just beyond some large trees. We kept a close eye on the ground, to make sure none of the spies were still hiding behind some of those trees. We were running silent, hoping they wouldn't notice us, not 'til we were right on top of them. Looks like we'd gotten there just in the nick of time. The men in black were dragging the Professor into the van. Looked like he was putting up a pretty good fight too, but there were three of the spies dragging him along. Must've been like Jimmy thought, they didn't need the Gravity Boxes, if they had the Professor.

This was another time the box didn't wait for orders. It was like it was not only reading my mind, but the Professor's too. The box sent out a ray of green light, that blasted the bad dudes about thirty feet away from the Professor. It just tossed them into the air like they were babies. They cried like babies too, all the way to the ground. None of them were hurt though, just seemed a little upset, especially the one who landed on the roof of the lab, and almost slid off of the side. I thought it might be a good idea to just zap up the Professor and split, but my Gravity Box had different ideas. Out of nowhere, the bad guys came pouring out of the lab, and the back of the house with their guns drawn. Before we could make anything happen, my box shot out with a wide blast of green lightening hitting all the weapons, and forced their guns to weigh about a thousand pounds, 'cause they dropped out of their hands, and no one could even lift them. They smashed into the dirt, sinking in about two or three feet, and just stayed there. One of those guys seemed to be trapped in the dirt by the gun that was now too heavy to lift.

"Did you do that?" Jimmy yelled to me.

"Not that I know of."

"Keep up the good work!"

"I said I..." didn't matter that I couldn't get it out I thought, 'cause I looked so cool just blasting the guns out of their hands. One of the bad dudes stuck his head out of the window of the second floor of the house, and we didn't see him. Lucky for us, the Gravity Box didn't wait for that, 'cause he had a rifle in his hands. Before we could even catch hold of his action, before even hearing the crack of the bullet being fired, I was flung out of the way. That made me knock against Jimmy, and knock him out of the way of the bullet too. Both me and Jimmy circled like we were riding a loop to loop, and came right back into position to shoot a bright green bolt of lightning right back at the guy in the window. Like all the others, his weapon went crashing to the to the ground. It didn't seem like he was thinking quick enough, 'cause he hadn't let go of the gun, and was now falling to the ground with it. Only the beam grabbed him too, and just before

203

he hit the ground. For a minute his body zoomed across the sky, and it looked like he was gonna crash into a tree. Then suddenly, he stopped in mid-air. For a second he just floated there, swimming in the green light. Then he started to fall. You could hear him scream all the way down. For spies, these guys were doing a lot of screaming that night. He fell until he got about two feet from the ground. All at once he stopped, floated for one more second, and dropped belly down in the dirt. A couple of his friends ran to help him up, like he'd actually fallen all the way. Some others were still trying to get the Professor into the van. You think they'd a learned their lesson by now. Everybody else there was running back into the house for safety. Tried to get the box to stop the guys at the van, but it was still acting with a mind of its own. The van was starting to pull away, and as much as I wanted to stop them, my box refused to listen. Instead a wide-angle beam shot out, and hit both the house and the lab.

"You stop them," I shouted to Jimmy, "I can't make it work!"

He didn't answer me; he just soared off to save the Professor. Could feel the wind off of him as he zoomed on by me, and after the van. The handlebars started to shake really bad now, as the green beam seemed to be stuck right onto the whole house and the lab. A couple of the guys inside were looking out and up to see what was happening. They didn't like what they were seeing. What was gonna happen next, their guess was as good as mine. Now it was the house that had started trembling, but the box had stopped. The shaking was real bad, and I thought the house was gonna fall apart. The guys in black, that I could see were clutching like crazy on to the sides of the windows, and looking up at me like I was the blame. It shook real bad for like a minute, and then the roof was the first thing to go. It just left the house, that's right. Just pulled the nails and glue, or whatever roofs are put on with, and sent it soaring into the air. Could still hear the spies inside screaming and carrying on, but so far no one had been hurt. Guess I'd of been doing a lot of screaming and yelling myself.

As the top of the house opened up, you could see all the men inside looking up. They looked so small, and somehow not dangerous anymore. On their tiny faces they looked scared, real scared. Some of them looked like ants crawling under the furniture. Just then a giant wave the light filled up the whole space, and sent everything it shined on up and out, so that it was falling into the sky. Yes falling into the sky. More guys started being tossed into the air. Now they were grabbing onto pieces of furniture, like they were in the ocean, and an old China closet was a lifeboat that was gonna keep them afloat. But since everything was flying upwards, it really didn't make any sense to grab hold of something else. They were clutching onto things that were already flying into the power of the light.

Then the house shook even more, and the box rumbled a few more times. Didn't know what to expect next, 'cause I definitely was no longer in control. I'd even stopped trying to put pictures in my head, and just started watching the fun. Like I said the box had stopped trembling, and the green beam now covered the whole house and the lab. At first just one brick loosened, and flew into the air. And I thought that's it, all that rumbling for one lousy brick. Boy was I wrong; the beam in a second turned a darker shade of green, and then it lifted two more bricks, then four. Now my eyes were glued to the action, while right in front of my face the whole building started to rumble and tumble, but not down to the ground, it was soaring into the air. Like giant rain drops in reverse every piece of the house began to pour into the sky. Every second each part was flying up faster and faster, zooming up into the air. Out of nowhere, the Professor's television set rocketed up, and just missed hitting my head. All of the bad dudes were scared out of their heads as they shot up into the sky, but still all I could do was watch. For a second I almost felt sorry for these creeps. In no time, nothing was left on the ground, but the basement. But still the beam just kept shooting out. Suddenly, the hot water heater blasted into the air like a rocket, pouring steam, and zooming into the sky. It got so far, and just started dangling up there like the rest of the stuff. Now everything was moving much slower. The rain of the Professor's stuff into the air had become a drizzle, and was coming to a standstill. All I could think was that this box had gone crazy on me again. Kept hoping that it wasn't gonna drop the house, and all these guys on their heads, 'cause they were now up higher than even me. About sixty feet away from where I was, one of the bad guys was calling out to me.

"Hey kid... kid, let me down, will you?"

"Come on kid, please," another called for help.

Even with all their begging, and me actually feeling sorry for them, 'cause I knew how it felt to be helpless up here, there was nothing that I could do. The box wasn't minding me. It had all gone crazy. AGAIN! It seemed to be doing everything that would've been done by me, but it still wasn't doing it for me, if you know what I mean? So I just shrugged my shoulders to them, and they called me some names that I'm not allowed to repeat, even if I knew what they meant. All right, so I knew what they meant, but you can't hear them anyway.

Just kept watching, but I still couldn't do anything about it, when a loud noise hit my ears. Sounded like a blender after you drop some ice into it. Had to look over my shoulder to see. Then there it was! Coming up fast on me was a huge helicopter. It had a big glass bubble on the front, but the sun was hitting it, and glaring kinda bright, so you couldn't see in. As it came closer, I was waiting for whoever it was to start shooting machine guns at me, or something. Had to get out of there. Put that picture in my head, but still nothing would happen, and I just stayed there floating in the air as helpless as those other guys were.

The helicopter was almost right on top of me. Darn! Where was Jimmy? Could've used some help right about then. Why'd I have to get the broken box again?

"Let's get out of here, will ya'," I shouted at the box, but it still wasn't listening to me, or reading my thoughts. The wind was strong at my back from the propeller that was blowing the air all around me, but instead of machine gun bullets, came a loud booming voice. Someone was shouting over a loudspeaker at me. Didn't know who it was though.

"Put those men down," the voice ordered.

Tried to turn to tell them what was going on, that I wasn't doing any of it, but it just wouldn't happen. My yelling could not be heard above the noise of the chopper blades.

"Put those men down now," the voice told me again, and he really sounded like he meant business.

Was waiting to get blasted right out of the sky. Then I thought maybe they'd leave me alone, just to save their own guys. Nah, I thought, that's not the way it happens in the movies. The bad guys always shoot everyone, even their own men, to keep the secret from falling into the wrong hands, or mostly the right hands. Which made me think, why would anyone want to work for these guys in the first place. Sure the guys in the chopper were probably just thinking of me as some punk kid, who had just ruined their plans. Kept looking back at the helicopter, trying to call out, but they just couldn't understand.

"Can't make it work," I shouted, but still the noise from the whirling blades was drowning me out. Next thing I heard was another voice. This one I knew.

"Son," it was my Dad. This time my head twisted real hard to look back at the chopper that had swung around, so that my father's face was looking out through the side door.

"Put those men down safely, please!" Dad sounded real nervous. Guess the reason for that was easy to know. Didn't want to have him hurt, but how could he know what was happening, that I wasn't really controlling the darn thing.

"Listen to your father Shawn," another voice came across the speaker.

Oh no! Didn't have to think about that one either, that was my Mom. Why'd they have to bring her along too? As much as I tried to turn my head, I couldn't see her. Guess she was sitting behind Dad, or somebody else in the chopper.

It was the Moment of Truth. That's what they call it in cowboy movies, when two guys are pointing guns at each other, and you're waiting for the hero to shoot the creep. Only in my case, they had the gun, and it was pointed right at my back. My gun was stuck in my holster, and wouldn't come out for nothing. Was gonna try to tell them one more time my problem, when I figured what was the use. No matter what I said, the box was just gonna keep those dudes floating in the air, like they were dangling from a mobile or something.

"SHAWN!" That was my Dad's voice again. If only he knew how much I wanted to obey him. Getting shot scared me, but what really had me feeling bad was that I could do nothing to help my parents. "PUT THOSE PEOPLE DOWN, NOW!" That time I didn't even look back at him, 'cause I knew I would only cry.

The chopper now started to move around to my side, like they wanted me to get a good look at my parents. Like they thought it could help change my mind or something. If only they knew how I wanted to do something, anything to make things all right. They were being real careful not to get in front of the green beam that like a giant waterfall was still pouring out all over the sky.

If only Jimmy would show up. That's the only hope that seemed left to me. Right now nothing else was gonna do any good; at least that's what I thought. Then all at once it happened. The color of the beam switched from a green one to a dark purple. Again, the box started shaking up a storm, but the storm wasn't rain and wind, it was people, and furniture, and pieces of the house.

Looked at the people in the chopper, and they looked at me. They were watching what was happening, and I pretended like whatever it was, I was doing it all on purpose. If they thought that I

209

could knock them out of the sky, or maybe that I was just plain crazy, maybe they'd be scared enough not to shoot me, or hurt my parents. Could see my Mom now, and it made me feel real bad for her, for both of my parents, 'cause it seemed like it was me that had caused all their troubles. Knew that Mom would never hold it against me, but I felt bad anyway.

The purple light was now filling the whole sky in front of me. Strange things were beginning to happen. Like for instance, everything inside the weird new light stopped moving altogether. The men, the furniture, the different bricks that had flown up into the air, seemed to freeze right on their spots, some higher than me. It was like they were stuck in ice, or something like that. A quick peek at the chopper let me know that everyone inside was awfully worried now, but just weren't saying anything anymore. Good, 'cause there really wasn't any answers, not from me anyway.

Then everything started shifting. Almost like a giant whirlpool. Now it was moving faster and faster, making more wind than even the chopper. First thing I felt was my hair blowing all over my head as everything, the house and all began to spin around the sky a hundred miles an hour. The wind from that was hitting the trees, and blowing leaves all over the place. It was like being in a hurricane. And what really had me worried was the chopper being knocked around the sky. My Mom and Dad were in there.

"STOP IT!" I yelled as loud as I could, but the stupid box wasn't listening at all that day. Where the heck was Jimmy? I grabbed even tighter onto the handlebars. That was so that the wind wouldn't blow me off of the Gravity Box. And then as fast as it had

210

started, the whirlpool in space slowed to a complete stop. It looked like everything inside the purple light had been jumbled up, and put into a different place. Now the bricks were just bobbing up and down in the air below everything else. The furniture and the men were all in the same positions they had been inside the house, only still floating up there as high as me, some even higher. And that rickety old roof, it was dangling over it all. The Gravity Box let go with another violent rumble, and then what happened next you wouldn't believe. The purple beam began to drop all of the bricks. Not fast, not like when it rained into the air, but slower. As they dropped down, each brick stacked perfectly on top of the basement wall, and started to make a line around the edge where the house had been. Like a bricklayer might do, only there was no bricklayer. There were just spurts of the purple ray of light charging the air, and directing each brick into the right spot.

After that the rocket water heater made a successful re-entry. That's astronaut talk for perfect parking job. The wall was being built all over again brick by brick. It was the same thing with the floorboards. They dropped right into place. The rain of house parts and furniture had reversed itself, and piece-by-piece the house was falling together again. The Gravity Box had remembered where it had picked up each and everything in the house, and now it was putting it right back in the same spot. The windows, the walls, even the guys under the furniture, who were still doing a lot of screaming, and not happy about any of it.

Above it all was the roof, now hovering up there like a giant tent all by itself, high above the rest of the house. It started to fall like everything else, but something was wrong. The roof began falling too fast, and looked like it was going to crash into the rest of the house. It was falling like it would've fallen if the purple beam hadn't been holding it up. It was plummeting like a meteor headed right at the rest of the house, and the helpless spies now trapped below looked like they were gonna get crushed. I closed my eyes, 'cause I really didn't want to see it. Then suddenly the Gravity Box churned, and shook like an old junker car that was on its last legs, and spurted out one gigantic flash of green light. Green was good, I thought, green was the color of light that I knew something about. Now all at once the roof slowed down like the rest of the stuff. After a minute when there was no crash, I had to look again. Beautiful, the beam had eased it to a halt. Like seconds before the roof would've smashed into the rest of the house, it stopped, and sealed itself into position with a perfect landing. Once that was done, the beam cut out instantly.

And people watching this must've thought that I was responsible for all of it, and I really didn't know if that was a good thing. Because let me tell ya', I looked like a real terror tossing the house and spies all over the place like they were rag dolls, and I didn't know if that was a good thing either. If they thought that I was crazy enough, I just might be able to get them to give me anything I wanted, and most of all I wanted by parents and my little sister back.

"That's a good boy," my Mom shouted over the loudspeaker on the chopper. "Now, put that machine down on the ground. Please son! We'll be with you right away. I've missed you baby!"

"Do what you're Mom's says son," my Dad added on.

And to tell the truth, I really didn't mind being called baby, even with all those guys around. It just made me so happy to be hearing her voice, my Dad's too. The only problem now, was should I really listen to my Mom. Sure both she and Dad had sounded serious enough. That didn't mean that I should give away probably our only chance against these guys. I think that's what Jimmy would have thought. The truth was, that the old Gravity Box wasn't going to let me do anything, but watch what it wanted to do, so maybe it knew something that I didn't.

"Jimmy, you dirt bomb, where are ya'?" I yelled that out at the sky, even though I knew Jimmy couldn't hear me. Didn't really mean the name-calling, just couldn't help it. I was just so scared, and Jimmy always knew what to do when things got really crazy. Although, things had never really been this crazy, maybe not for anyone.

"Put the machine down son," somebody said, only it wasn't my Dad, it was some other guy. "Everything is going to be alright now."

Should I believe him or not. Thought long and hard on that one, about two seconds. Came up with the answer, no! Even if I could control the Gravity Box, these guys were probably the ones who took my parents hostage in the first place. And why would I ever trust someone like that?

But while my head was spinning, trying to come up with a way out of this mess, the box decided to start handling things on its own. Without any orders from me, it turned right towards the chopper. They had changed position, and with the sun no longer hitting the glass bubble of the chopper I could see in through the windshield now. There was still a glare, but there were a few of faces that I could make out staring right at me. They all looked scared to death, including Dad's, and Mom's.

"No," I screamed at the box afraid that it was gonna do something crazy again.

"No, turn it away," shouted one of the men over the microphone. "What are you doing, turn it away!"

Any second a beam was gonna come shooting out at that chopper. My Mom and Dad were on it, and there was nothing that I could do to stop it. Then I thought, maybe I could save them if I let go of the box. Maybe if no one was holding on, it would just fall to earth with me. It was a long fall, and I would probably get killed, but then maybe my parents would have a chance. But if these guys were really killers, Mom and Dad had no chance at all without me and the box. I really didn't know what to do. There were a thousand ideas bouncing around inside of my head again, and they all sounded like they could end in disaster.

CHAPTER 15. THE WHOLE TRUTH AND NOTHING BUT...

Like I told ya' none of what was happening seemed good. Should I trust the guys in the helicopter? Should I let go of the box, drop a thousand feet or so, and hope to land on some soft grass? That was actually the best plan, 'cause the Gravity Box was now making all the decisions, and it seemed like I was just along for the ride.

A couple of the spies that were back on the ground came running out of the house. Looked down quick, and saw one of them trying to pick up his gun, but it was still too heavy to lift. Had to get my mind away from them, had to try and get the Gravity Box to turn away from that chopper, but my brain, and the machine just weren't connecting any longer. Saw the pilot trying to swing around out of the path of where the beam might shoot. As he spun the helicopter, the Gravity Box turned to follow the choppers every movement.

"Stop," I begged the box, but it still wouldn't listen.

"Son, son...." that guy in the chopper called to me again, "please turn the machine away from the helicopter," and he was acting like I had a choice. Then he must've been so nervous that he left the microphone on while he talked to the pilot, or one of the others with him.

"We're gonna have to shoot him down!"

"No, please, don't," my Mom screamed out. Sounded like she was gonna cry. Maybe she was already crying. We must be a big family of criers.

"Come on Jimmy, please," I begged to the sky again hoping somehow he would hear me, and come riding, or better yet, flying to the rescue. I was no longer trying to explain to the people in the chopper, 'cause the sound of the whirling blades was still drowning out all my words. I was a sitting duck, but so were they. Any second the Gravity Box could take another shot at them or the spies down below, and we all knew it. The guys down on the ground were still running for cover. And if the guys in the chopper did take a shot at me, the Gravity Box might not just move me out of the way. That was the thing that scared me the most. It was like the Gravity Box had a brain inside that was programmed to protect me or itself no matter what. And what if "no matter what" meant crashing the chopper with my parents inside? Right then it really didn't seem to matter what old Shawn wanted.

"Let me explain to him," could hear my Dad say. The mic in the chopper was still on, and this was a one-way conversation that I wasn't enjoying.

"There's no time," the other voice said, and that fast some type of rifle barrel came sliding out of the chopper.

"He's just a child," my Mom cried out, but that didn't seem to stop them. I guess I was just a kid, but at the same time just old enough to get shot out of the sky.

Just like before my eyes closed tight. And that too didn't matter if I wanted them to or not. They just squeezed shut tight, like my hands on the handlebars of the box. My fingers were now starting to lose their strength, 'cause all the blood had started going other places, like my thumping heart, and my stomach now turning into knots. And then all at once there was another scream, but it wasn't me. I expected it to be me, but it wasn't. When I got the nerve up to peek through my one eye that wasn't glued shut, the beam had blasted green again. Like a thunderbolt, it darted across the sky hitting the rifle, and only the rifle. Like magic it flew into the air. Whoever was holding the rifle was pulled out of the chopper, and into the sky with it. I would have never believed that so many adults cried like babies. He was now flying through space higher than the chopper. Everybody else was watching him as he went sailing through the air. He was about a couple of hundred more feet up, when he made a big mistake, or lost his grip and let go of the rifle. He started screaming even louder on the way down. His legs kicked and his arms flapped, like he was trying to fly on his own. It looked bad for him. Had to try and help him, even if he was one of those creeps. So, my eyes closed tight again, and I tried to imagine him floating on a giant green cloud. But still he kept nose diving to the ground.

"Listen to me," I screamed to the box, and then closed my eyes again. I saw the falling guy as clear as day dancing through the air. There was a slight tremble in the handlebars, and when I looked the green beam had caught him right in mid-air. And I thought, maybe I was in control of the Gravity Box again. Tried to see myself moving over to that guy, but not too close, and once again the box had done what I wanted.

"Tell them to land, and to let my Mother and Father go!"

"Listen son..." he started to say.

"I ain't your son," I yelled at him.

It seemed hard for him bobbing around in mid-air as he started to fumble for something in his pocket.

"Don't do it!"

He took my warning seriously, 'cause he pulled his hand away real quick like. "Only going to pull out my wallet," he explained carefully.

"Why!"

"Because I'm an officer for the Department of Justice."

"So?"

"So," he sounded surprised.

"Yeah, so! Does that mean ya' have a right to kidnap my Mom and Dad, and try to run over me and Jimmy, tie us up in the basement, and rough up Ricky." I know I was rambling on, but all the anger just exploded out of me all at once.

"Huh?"

"Don't huh me, ya' know what I'm talking about!"

"You got us all wrong son; we just rescued your parents."

Wasn't sure if I should believe him. Looked over at the chopper. My Mom and Dad looked all right. They weren't tied up, or nothing like that. Maybe the guy was for real.

"Aww, Jimmy, where the heck are ya'?" Really wanted to talk this thing out with him.

"What," asked the dude from the Justice Department.

"Nothin'!"

Before we could say anything else my wish was granted. Gliding across the trees came the black van. Holding tight to the top was our friend Bad Guy Number 1 that we had left on top of the big oak.

"What's happening here," Jimmy yelled to me.

"Where ya' been?"

"I figured it wasn't fair to the birds leaving this guy at the top of the tree, and I didn't want the Professor to get too far, so I circled back and…"

I really didn't care what had happened, I was just glad to see Jimmy. I was sure he'd know what to do.

"This guy says he's working for the government."

"Did he say which government," Jimmy made a little joke, which he didn't usually do. Guess being one of the most powerful kids on the planet made you cocky.

While I was ready to fill in Jimmy on everything that had happened, for a minute he got careless, maybe what you'd call stupid. Never thought I'd be saying that about him. While he was looking at me, the van with the spy boss on top of it was floating close by to Jimmy. Without any warning, the spy boss pulled a second gun from underneath his pant leg, dove off of the floating van, and grabbed hold of Jimmy in midair.

"Look out," I tried to get out as soon as I saw him make the jump, but I was too late. Blondie had hold of Jimmy, and was pointing the gun right into his side. Jimmy let go with a loud cry as the spy boss struggled to keep hold of him, and keep himself from falling.

"Get off of me," Jimmy shouted out, but the spy boss wasn't listening to him at all.

"Shut up kid," the spy boss ordered Jimmy, and then he called out loud to me from across the sky. "If you're friend means anything to you, you will not make any attempts to save him with your gravity device."

"But…" I tried to get out.

"No buts," yelled back the spy boss. "I am in charge now. If you attempt to save him, my gun will go off. I don't think you're that fast."

Me and Jimmy looked right into each other's eyes. I could tell how scared he was.

"Sorry Shawn," Jimmy said, and looked down at the ground so far below.

"Well what will it be, do I get the gravity device, or does you little buddy get a hole in his side?"

"Shawn don't try and save me," Jimmy's voice shook when was saying those words.

"Shut up," said the spy boss, "I'm in charge now."

Jimmy kept looking me right in the eye, and then he said it, "Not yet."

With those words Jimmy let go of the Gravity Box, and started to fall to the ground along with the spy boss, and the other box. The spy boss lost his grip on Jimmy right away as he was going down. I could hear both of their voices filled with fear as they kept falling faster and faster. As he was headed towards the ground, the spy boss spun in the air, and was firing his gun at me. Guess it was hard for him to take good aim speeding towards the dirt, but I thought I felt some bullets whizzing on by me. Like a second later, the van started to plummet to the woods below with more screams filling the air.

"Now," I heard Jimmy's voice calling to me as he was falling to the earth like a burning meteor.

"WHAT?" I shouted back to him.

"SAVE ME NOW!" Though he was like a thousand feet down, I heard that clear enough.

I understood right away what Jimmy had meant when he said, "don't save me...yet." So, I knew it was time to save him now. Just like the other times, I didn't have to even think about it. The green beam from the Gravity Box shot out, and blasted its way across the sky hitting both Jimmy, the spy boss, and the other box. For a minute I thought that the box had forgotten about the van, but no, it too stopped in midair, and just seemed bob up and down for a minute. For like a second it all just floated in the air. I could see that the spy boss was going to try and shoot Jimmy again, and again without any thought from me, the beam let go of the spy boss, who once more was headed towards the ground. He was pretty far away, but I could tell that was him screaming again. The beam let him land soft enough, but the gun must've weighed a ton at this point, because it fell to the ground, and trapped his hand and him in the dirt. Then the second box just floated next to Jimmy, and he was once more in control, and on his way back up to be with me.

"Thanks man," Jimmy said. "Glad you got my meaning."

Didn't have time to think about any of that, we had another big problem in front of us.

"Jimmy, they got my Mom and Dad in that chopper. What should I do?"

While everybody was floating around in the air, and the chopper kept whizzing its blades, Jimmy put his head down to think. That was always a good sign. Who was I trying to kid? Sometimes that was a good sign; sometimes it meant we were really in deep trouble.

"Got it," he said.

"Good boy," I said, "good boy!"

Then he took the van, and stuck in on the top of the biggest tree he saw. The guys inside were calling to us, and begging to be put down, but who was listening. The van crushed a few of the smaller branches, but then it just wobbled up there, while everyone inside I'm guessin' was trying to stay perfectly still.

"What about the birds?" I laughed to Jimmy. He smiled back. "And the guns, what about their guns," 'cause I really wanted to know about that.

"I let them know if I fell, they would fall, and since nobody wanted to fall..."

"But spy boss pulled his gun on you," I said.

"Guess he just didn't care about the others."

He stopped with his story, and now let the Gravity Box do all the talking.

Next the beam opened the side door to the van, and picked the Professor out, and brought him right over to us.

"Put me down," he yelled at us all the way. "You know how I hate heights!"

"Professor Burkhardt," Jimmy started to say, but when the Professor saw the guy from the justice department, who was floating near to us he started talking to him.

"Thank goodness you arrived; I was beginning to think you would never get here."

"Then this guy's all right," I asked.

"Of course not, he works for the government, but he's come to rescue us!"

Could feel a swallow sliding down my throat. Here I'd been messing around with real G. Men, who were actually trying to help us out. They had probably saved my parents. Just hoped that what I did wasn't treason, or nothing like that. Jimmy looked at me and me back at him, and then we put everything down on the ground. Then we only had one problem. That was who we were in the most trouble with. Was it Mom and Dad for running away, the government for almost shooting down one its aircraft, and throwing one of its agents out of it; or the Professor for flying him up a lot higher than he'd ever wanted to go. It was a big problem, but one I just happened to luck out on. First of all Mom and Dad were glad just having me back, and to be alive. They were amazed by what they had seen, and both still thought they were dreaming. Well Jimmy's parents, that was gonna be a different story. Chances were since they didn't actually see any of this, they weren't gonna believe a word of it. Probably have Jimmy locked away in some crazy house, and try to put me there too. Could probably have anyone who knew the truth put there with us. Yeah, we were gonna have a lot of company. The government guys forgave us real easy, 'cause we had captured some really bad dudes. Plus, we'd shown them how well the Gravity Box really worked. All we had to do for them was promise to keep the whole thing hush hush. Top secret, you know? The only one who wasn't happy, besides the captured spies, was the Professor. While the Gravity Boxes were being packed away to be sent to a government lab, he explained his whole story to us.

It seems that for years the Professor had worked for the Government in a top secret, what was the word he used, a yeah, "capacity." After his work was done, 'cause he still had a lot of what he called classified stuff in his head, he still was kept an eye on by the Department of Justice and guys like that. Guess the foreign agents must've been able to find him too. He said they probably weren't looking for the gravity machine, 'cause that was his own idea, and until me and Jimmy came along nobody else knew about it. So they just came across it while trying to steal some other ideas he might of had. The Professor figured that they were just waiting until it was perfected, and then swipe it and Professor too. There were still a lot of crazy ideas inside his head, so I guess a lot of governments wanted a piece of the Professor's brain.

So, you see Jimmy was right. That night we first saw the men in black, they weren't putting in the bugs. They were taking them out. They didn't want to leave any trace of ever being there. The Professor also said that since we knew it all, that the bad guys probably didn't want to leave any trace of us either. Pretty scary, huh? Oh, and as for me having the broken box. We had that all wrong too. The box that the spy had was the one that the Professor had kept out to be fixed. We had actually grabbed hold of the good machine.

"It was designed," the Professor told us, "to compute bad situations, and make them good!"

"Huh," I said.

"The Gravity Box can also read your subconscious mind, and make corrections based on what it is seeing in you."

"My subterranean mind…" I tried to get out.

"Subconscious mind," Jimmy corrected me. Think he loved doing that. " Well in your case maybe subterranean," he laughed, "We'll explain it later to him Professor," Jimmy said.

Jimmy said it worked something like this; when I couldn't think fast enough, an electric eye or something shoved all of the information in my head into the computer inside the box, and saved the day. Also, the good box was fixed so that it can't' do bad things, or make mistakes like before.

"The gravity machine is limited only by evil and stupidity," the Professor said.

"Guess that means that the Gravity Box was smarter than me?"

"Not at all," said the Professor. It just didn't have to wait for your thoughts to become conscious, but if those thoughts are evil, the machine has a logic system that will not allow it produce harm."

"Huh?' I really wasn't getting this.

Anyway, it was a good thing that the Gravity Box was watching out for me, or who knows what could have happened. The Professor figured that would be best, or people might go crazy, or hurt themselves having so much power. The only trouble with that is, that the broken box could do all sorts of bad things, and the computer inside would let it happen. That means that the spy boss could've ripped us apart. Yet it did let us make him fall from the cloud.

"Maybe it knew our intentions were good," said Jimmy, "but how is that possible?" The Professor just smiled. "Professor," Jimmy asked again.

"That," the Professor said," is a secret greater than the power of levitation. All I can tell you is, that I have given the gravity machine intelligence, and the ability to rationalize clearly, also the computer inside the gravity machine connected with the computer inside your head," he pointed to his own head. "Instilled with those qualities made the choices simple. As with men who possess these qualities, the machine could only act towards the greater good of man." Across the room he looked sadly at the one Gravity Box being packed away by the government agents. "Once dissected, and its memory erased, it could do great harm." Then he shook his head, and looked down at the ground real sad.

"What's wrong Professor," I said.

"It's just that my little toy was designed to be an aid to man, to keep planes from crashing to the earth, to allow people to leap from burning buildings, and survive."

"Well, can't it still be," I asked him.

"It can," said Jimmy, "but what the Professor's trying to say is that it won't!"

"Instead of making planes land safely, it might make them crash. It will take missiles, and send them back on their own people; it can create tidal waves, crush buildings under their own weight, and suffocate people in their own gravity. I was a fool," the Professor said.

"Then don't give it to anybody," I told him.

Slowly the Professor looked out the window again. Below the window the first Gravity Box was being placed into the back of a military van.

"It's too late already, they have confiscated my invention."

"How can they do that," I yelled.

"National security," said the Professor.

"With that excuse you can get away with almost anything," Jimmy put in his two cents.

"Now I wish that you boys could have destroyed the boxes, so that no trace remained; so that it would be as if it... it..." The Professor couldn't get the words out, and he looked like he was gonna cry.

"Never existed," Jimmy filled in the blanks. "Is that what you really want Professor?"

The Professor just nodded his head, but did not answer with words. Me and Jimmy just looked at each other. From the outside, the men had come back into the lab, and had carried out the second box. I looked back at the Professor. He looked awful sad. Jimmy put his head down, and it looked like he was thinking again. Somehow, I knew that that meant trouble. And if you've been paying attention up to now, you know the same thing. Then he looked back up at me.

"No," I said.

"But you don't even know what I'm gonna say!"

"Don't care, just got out of the biggest mess of my life, and I'm looking like a hero."

"We can do it," he said, looking me right in the eye.

"No!"

"What are you two talking about," the Professor looked over at us.

"This is the government," I said.

"Don't listen to him Professor," Jimmy said.

"Listen to what? I still don't know what you're talking…" the Professor tried to get out.

"The government," I said again. I said it louder this time, and hoped that Jimmy was hearing me.

"Keep your voice down," Jimmy said.

"THE GOVERNMENT…" but nobody seemed to be listening to me.

"Down… down…" Jimmy tried to get me to shut my yap. "And they're doing wrong…"

"Don't they call that treason, or something?"

"Treason," the Professor said. He sounded unsure. That wasn't helping me feel any better.

"Voice down," Jimmy was now even ordering the Professor. Then it was back to me. "What I'm saying…" Jimmy tried to go on.

"Or something like that," the Professor cut him off. Not sure if Jimmy was talking about treason.

"Jimmy," I tried again, but he just wasn't listening.

"Sabotage," said the Professor.

"What," I said.

"I think they call it sabotage..." the Professor said again.

"How," said Jimmy.

"That's what destroying those boxes would be called. Maybe even sabotage and treason," the Professor shrugged.

None of this was making me feel good.

"If people all over the world get crushed, it'll be your fault," Jimmy tried to put a head trip on me.

"We'll never get away with it!"

"But we're the most powerful kids in the universe."

"Not without those boxes! And I thought it was just this planet."

"What", Jimmy looked confused.

"I thought we were only the two most powerful kids on this planet."

"Aw shut up," Jimmy shouted at me. Then he looked down kind of sad like a hurt puppy. It's gonna be hard on my own."

"Aww, don't do this to me!" Knew what he was doing, he was using psychology on me, and knowing that it was psychology, didn't mean that I didn't fall for it most of the time. It usually worked, but I wasn't gonna fall for it this time.

"Boys! Boys! Boy!" The Professor tried to stop us.

Stopping me was not the problem. Jimmy was the problem.

"When's the last time they shot a kid for sabotage," Jimmy said.

"When's the last time one stole an atomic bomb?"

"Maybe they call it espionage," said the Professor.

Espionage, that was another word I didn't like.

"Please stop helping Professor, besides I think espionage is more about stealing state secrets," then Jimmy looked back at me, "doesn't even belong to them," Jimmy threw back in my face.

"Boys! Boys! Boys!"

"But..." I was running out of buts.

"It really doesn't belong to them," the Professor slipped in like he was beginning to go along with Jimmy's argument. Then he looked at me sadly. "The world's not really ready for it. We have to develop a lot more, become saner. Then maybe, but not for a long, long time."

Now I was beginning to feel like a real creep. Tidal waves, people suffocating, and planes crashing all over the place because of me.

"But of course you boys are not responsible for the problems of the world..." the Professor shook his head like he was coming out of his daydream.

"I got a plan," Jimmy said.

"You've always got a plan!"

"I've gotten us this far, didn't I?"

"No, no, I can't allow it," said the Professor, Jimmy acted as if he didn't hear any of it, and began telling us his plan.

We'd already taken on foreign agents, how much trouble could one more country be? Even James Bond would've quit by now. Well maybe not James Bond.

CHAPTER 16. DID WE REALLY THINK IT'D WORK?

The plan was a simple one, and should work easy. Who was I kidding, just myself? No, not even myself. It was the craziest thing I'd ever heard! Was beginning to think we were both crazy. Jimmy for thinking it, and me for going along with all the craziness.

First of all, the whole thing was depending on how good an actor the Professor was. Oh, I forgot to tell you, that the Professor seemed to be as crazy as the rest of us, 'cause he was going along for the ride.

We had to move fast, 'cause the two Gravity Boxes were already loaded into the back of the military van. There was a little time left, 'cause the agents were outside talking to my parents. I guess telling them the same things they had told us. That was to keep our big yaps shut about the Gravity Boxes, and fighting the spies, and saving the world, and all that junk. Open their traps once about any of it, and we'd all end up in big trouble. It was all the bull being slung around that gave us the time we needed to set up.

Outside they still had the chopper, and that wasn't good. It would probably be following the military van all the way to where it was going. I'm talking top security, that kinda stuff. There were only four agents left. Jimmy figured two would go in the chopper, two in the van. They had two more vans, but they had been used to take the guys in black away from the lab. And let me tell ya', we were glad to see the last of them. Think they were kinda glad to be getting out of there in one piece.

The plan could work, but first they'd have to believe the Professor's acting job. If that didn't work, we'd be shot down before we got out of the starting gate, and I mean really shot down. It all depended on that.

"Oh my chest," the Professor let loose right in the middle of the lab. He followed that right up with, "I can't breath." One of the agents ran right over to see what was going on. The Professor was holding onto his chest, and breathing in and out real heavy. It wasn't a bad acting job. It wouldn't have got the Professor no awards or nothing.

"What's wrong Professor Burkhardt?" the agent asked, worried like. That's when the Professor really started pouring it on. He did a lot of gasping, and asked the agent to help him to a chair.

"My pills, please, quick I don't have long... It could be fatal... The light... the light, everything's growing dim…" The Professor wasn't too bad in the beginning, but he was startin' to lay the acting on a little thick.

"Where's the pills?" the agent looked at me and Jimmy. We just shook our heads like we didn't know. The agent knelt down real quick next to the Professor, "Professor Burkhardt, where are your pills?"

"AHHHH..." the Professor moaned, "the pain, the pain..." Just then I looked over to see Jimmy looking down over the agent's shoulder at the Professor. Jimmy was holding his hands over the left side of his chest, trying to get the Professor to do the same. He'd obviously forgotten which side of his chest his heart was on. The Professor caught on fast enough though, and started sliding his hand across to the other side.

"The pain's traveling... it's traveling," he said.

"The pills, where are the pills?" the one agent tried to get out of the Professor again.

That's when the Professor pulled his best acting out of the hat. He started coughing, and pretended trying to catch his breath. Then he let his eyes roll up into his head. It looked pretty good, to me anyway. What was really important was that the agent was buying the act.

Then the agent cursed, almost like he was blaming the Professor for being sick. Right then he turned to us again. "Get me one of my men to help find those pills. Go! Go!"

Sounded good to us. We were off and running to the window. Out of the corner of my eye I could see Jimmy smiling as we ran to window.

"It ain't over yet," I whispered.

"Shut up," Jimmy said. Maybe he thought I was being a killjoy. It was his party, so I just shut my trap.

"Hurry, help!" Jimmy yelled out the window.

"The Professor's dying!" I tried that next.

"Not so thick," Jimmy looked at me.

"That was pretty good acting," that's what I said, 'cause that's what I thought.

"You're a worse actor than the Professor!"

"Well if..."

For a second we'd actually forgotten about the Professor, and about the plan. It was like for that one minute all we could think about was how good or how bad of an actor I was, and that got me mad. We looked at each other real hard putting on our meanest faces.

"What's wrong?" one of the other agents had come over to the window from the outside, and now was standing right underneath us. My Mom and Dad were not far away.

"Is everything alright," my Dad called out.

"Ah...ah..." I said.

"The Professor's sick, he needs help," cried Jimmy. Jimmy was playing it good, real good.

"Oh my God," my Mom cried out.

"Please... please... He needs help!" I pretended to cry, couldn't get the tears though. Still I think my acting was just as real looking as Jimmy's.

"Yeah, he can't breathe," Jimmy added on. Almost believed him myself. Maybe Jimmy was the better actor.

"We'll be right in," the agent outside told us. Then he turned to the other guy by the helicopter, "Ray, bring in that oxygen tank from the chopper, pronto!"

And they were both off and running. So far things were working pretty good. While the one guy was busy getting first aid stuff from the chopper, the other one had rushed into the lab.

"What's the trouble?" he asked and stopped, when he saw the Professor slouched in the chair gasping like he was struggling for his last breath.

"Pills, I'm looking for pills!" Those guys were yelling to each other now.

"What kind of..."

"Check the medicine closet, check out everything!" He then went right back reassuring the Professor, "It's going to be all right Professor Burkhardt, take slow deep breaths, and try to stay calm."

While that one stayed with the Professor, the two others started opening doors, searching through cabinets, anywhere that a pill could hide. One of the guys pulled out a pack of pills the Professor kept for sour stomach from underneath counter, and held them up.

"This anything?"

"That's not it, you idiot. You boys stop standing there and give us a hand."

"How, 'bout, if I check the bathroom in the house," Jimmy said.

"Good idea," the first agent said.

Out of nowhere my Mom and Dad ran in.

"What's wrong?" my Mom had already started bawling without knowing why. She was like that. Always crying at weddings, funerals, and sad television commercial. Any excuse to cry she would jump on.

"It's okay ah..." I started to tell her, but Jimmy cut me off.

"It's the Professor," Jimmy said, "looks like he's having the big one!"

"Oh my God" my Mom cried out again. She started bawling all the way now, and that was a flood that wouldn't be easy to stop.

"Get that woman out of here!" one of the agents shouted.

While my Dad was looking at the agent all confused like, Jimmy grabbed me by the arm.

"We'll check out the house," Jimmy called out as we ran out of the lab.

"Can I help?" my Dad called to us.

We both stopped dead in our tracks. There was a moment when neither of us had an answer. Then it hit me.

"We know where the Professor keeps all his junk Dad, you stay here, and calm down Mom." That seemed to satisfy him, and make him feel useful all at the same time.

Both of us were off and running to the house, but that's not where we stopped. The Professor was doing a good job when we left, and we were both sure he'd keep them busy while we did what we had to do. On the way through the house Jimmy picked up his special briefcase. Now I was gonna find out what the other stuff in there was all about.

"Why'd ya' have to tell my Mom all that stuff?" I asked Jimmy as we jogged along.

"Did you want to tell her the truth, that we were about to steal the greatest secret weapon since the nuclear bomb? That would have gone down just great."

He was right; they would've stopped us right there and then. My family wasn't big into letting me do dangerous stuff, even though it was my business.

"But ya' didn't have to go and get her all upset, did ya'?"

"It worked out perfectly, she's a bigger distraction than the Professor."

Don't think he was complimenting my Mom, but she did have everyone running around crazy. And it kept my Dad busy while we went off to save the world again.

Went through the door at the rear of the house, and hoped no one would see us. It was not gonna be easy. Standing outside, not far from the van was another G. Man that seemed to be keeping an eye on things. Jimmy pulled me back quick like to the side of the house, so we wouldn't be seen.

"Darn," he said, but still trying to keep it low.

"What are we gonna do," I said, because I really thought it was all over at that point.

Jimmy put his head down, and thought real hard. "Shawn, you've got to distract him."

"How the heck am I gonna do that?"

"Go tell him what's going on."

"Huh?"

"Not huh, go tell him what's going on…"

I was kinda confused at this point. "I don't know," I tried to get out.

"Let him know what's happening with the Professor," Jimmy said. "Let him think you're all upset, and you need to talk to an adult."

"You mean lie to him?"

"Shawn we're in the middle of a top secret military heist. Of course, you're gonna lie to him."

"But…" that's all I got out.

"Do you really think one little white lie is going to make it worse?" I was thinking on it when, "Just make sure he's got his back to the van." That's when Jimmy shoved me out from behind the house.

The G Man spotted me right away, as I almost tripped over a rock coming around the corner, while Jimmy stayed hidden behind the house.

"Is there something wrong kid," he said, as I ran closer.

"It's just the Professor… I'm pretty upset, I hope he's okay." The thoughts in my head were racing by a million a minute, as I was trying to think of what to say next.

"What's going on in there anyway?" the G Man asked me.

"It's Professor Burkhardt," those were the first words that popped into my head.

"I just asked you what's going on," and the way he said it was more out of him being curious, than actually caring about the Professor or me.

While we were talking, I remembered that Jimmy wanted me to have that guy looking away from the van. So I put my head down sad like, and walked past him, so he had to turn to look at me, and away from the van.

"It's just that he's my friend, and I'm real worried about him."

"Yeah I got that much," the G Man seemed like he was getting annoyed with me dragging the story out.

As I turned back to look at him, I could see Jimmy still carrying the briefcase, sneaking out to the back of the van where they had put the Gravity Boxes. Seeing that only made me more nervous.

"It's just that the Professor's old, and we've been friends for a while," I was just trying to think of things to say at this point, 'cause it seemed like my brain just didn't want work that night. The main thing I was thinking about was Jimmy trying to break into the back of the van just a few feet away. All I could see was Jimmy trying to shove something, looked like the fishing line or string through the small opening at the top of the window.

"Then maybe you should go back inside, and keep an eye on the old guy." The G Man just wanted to get rid of me now.

"Really nice weather, huh," I came back. I was already running out of things to say to this guy.

"What?" the G Man looked at me oddly.

"I mean it was a little chillier earlier." I was sounding dumber by the second. "Just wish I had a jacket back then…" my brain was scrambling for things to say, and I had no idea what was gonna come out next.

Behind him I could see Jimmy still playing with the back of the van. The G Man must have noticed me looking, because he did the worst possible thing, and turned. Jimmy was on the ball, and quickly stepped to the side of the van where he couldn't be seen.

As the guy started to look, I was still racing inside of my head trying to think, think, think of other things to say.

While he was turned, he kept talking to me, but didn't bother to look away from the van.

"I mean Mom's always yelling at me, I'm gonna catch my death of a cold."

It was then he turned back to me. "Did you see something over there?"

"My parents brought me a nice jacket for my birthday, but I never wear it." The stupid stuff just kept pouring out.

"I said did you see something?"

"Ahhh," I shook my head real nervous like.

Now he just kept walking to the other side of the van. He kept talking to me, but wasn't looking at me as he as he moved.

"I said did you see something?" This time he sounded really annoyed with me.

"Ah no," I said, but this wasn't stopping him as walked back to right where Jimmy was hiding. We're goners, I thought.

One more thing crossed my mind to say. "Did you ever get to meet the President?" I yelled at him, but he wasn't stopping. "I thought I saw a rabbit," I tried to stop him again, but this guy wasn't interested in rabbits, the President, or even my new jacket. He was just about on top of where I last saw Jimmy. Right near me was a rock. I picked it up. We were really in trouble now, and I was shaking in my shoes. As the G Man was about to look around the other side of the van, I threw the rock right near his foot, and screamed. "There it goes!"

The G Man turned, and looked really mad at me. "What is your problem kid?" he looked back, and started to move quick like towards me.

"Its the rabbit," I called back to him. "He just ran right in front of you, didn't you see it."

"What were you tossing rocks at it for?"

"Thought I could scare it away," I came right back at him.

"They're not dangerous you know." He was now looking at me like I was just crazy.

"Didn't want to take any chances," which was the dumbest thing I had said to the G Man since we started talking.

"Look kid, did you land on your head when you were flying that thing."

"You never know what they're thinking," I said, now sounding crazier, and more stupid with every word. I mean I had lied before, but never this bad.

"What?"

"The rabbits," I came right back at him. I would never hurt a rabbit, but honest, I couldn't think of anything else to say. "Anyway, you were telling me about the President," I said to him.

"I never said anything about the President." Now he was really annoyed. "Hey kid, this has been fun, but you have to go back into the house now."

"But," I tried to get out.

"Go," he ordered, and I began to walk back to the house slow like. I knew if he kept his eye on me he'd see Jimmy too. Just had to get him looking the other way, so I began running off to the side.

I screamed out loud again. "Look out, there's another one!"

"Another what?" the G Man yelled.

"Another rabbit!"

241

I bent down real quick, and picked up a second rock. It was then that I went chasing after the second imaginary monster rabbit.

"They're not dangerous," the G Man yelled at me, as I ran away from the van to give Jimmy time to get out of there. As the G Man was watching me, Jimmy began to move back towards the house. That's when we heard it.

"Get him out to the chopper," somebody said as the door to the lab swung open.

We also could hear the Professor yelling at them. "I don't want to fly; I don't want to fly!"

"Hey, what are you boys doing over there," said one of the guys coming out the door with the Professor.

Just then the G Man I was talking to, turned back to see Jimmy for the first time.

"What the…" I heard him start to say, as Jimmy ran up to me still carrying the briefcase.

"Let's split!" Jimmy yelled at me.

And we were off and running again. We were getting pretty good at it too.

"Get those kids!" Not even looking back, we could tell we were being chased. They didn't have quiet feet like the other agents, so it was easy to hear them running up behind us.

"Come back here," we heard one of them call, but that hadn't stopped us yet today. I took a quick look to see one of the G Men pulling out his gun, and I heard a click like it was about to be fired.

"Get down!" I yelled at Jimmy.

"Put that way," somebody ordered, and I guess he was telling the guy with the gun to put it back in his holster.

The briefcase was slowing us down, but we had a good head start. Wasn't daring to look back again, just listened to the stomping of footsteps coming up fast behind us.

"Forget them," one guy called out, and all at once me and Jimmy were the only ones running. After a few more steps we stopped to check on what was happening. That was simple, the two guys after us had quit the chase. Jimmy nodded his head, and we started walking back to the lab.

"What are we doing?" because I really didn't know.

"We're going back to the lab."

"Why, they'll be waiting for us!"

Jimmy didn't answer, he just kept walking back towards the lab.

"Can you at least clue me in on what we're doing?" he still didn't answer me, but kept walking. "This is crazy!"

"I want to see how they're getting the Professor out of there."

"What's that gonna..."

"If they use the chopper to get him out..."

"But he hates heights," I tried to get out.

"If they use the chopper, then we have to go with Plan B."

"There's a Plan B..."

"The helicopter not following the van gives us our shot."

"It does!"

"Shhh," Jimmy warned me. We were close to the lab.

We got hidden behind some trees, and watched whatever was going on. All four guys were helping the Professor onto the chopper. My Mom and Dad had just come out of the lab, and were just watching on, worried like. The Professor was still coughing and gagging, looking like a real pro actor by now. The agents on the scene were still too close, if we tried to get into the van now, they'd catch us for sure, and if they couldn't catch us, they would shoot us if they thought we were trying to get to the Gravity Boxes. Knowing how important they were, they'd have no choice. It was so strange, how in just a few minutes we had gone from being real heroes who had saved the world from a terrible disaster, to being considered dangerous criminals ourselves.

Jimmy then explained Plan B to me. It was the first I had heard it, and it was just as crazy as plan A. We would still look like criminals, still probably be shot, and we were dangerously close to getting grounded for the rest of our lives. The van would have to ride along the one road going away from the Professor's place, before it could pull out onto the major highway. If we ran all the way, there was a short cut through the woods that would let us beat them to the point near the main road. That was if they didn't start out too soon, and didn't drive too fast. Jimmy guessed with what they were carrying, they'd be moving kinda slow and safe like.

We were running as fast as we could. I was carrying the briefcase now, and it was banging into my leg all the way, so I had to keep switching sides. That way I wouldn't get bruised up any worst than I already was from a long day of battling bad guys. Was gonna tell Jimmy to hold onto it for a while, but I'm a way better runner than he is.

"This is crazy," I told him, which I was sure he already knew.

"Keep runnin'," he had heard all my arguments before.

"Suppose they run ya' over?"

"Keep runnin'!"

Which wasn't easy, cause my feet kept pounding and pounding into the ground, and my legs felt like they were about to explode. It suddenly hit me, that I hadn't eaten, or had anything to drink in hours. My throat was dry, my stomach cramped, and my lungs felt like they were on fire. Was even gettin' a little dizzy. And it was strange; being so close to be being shot, and all I could think about was that leftover crumb cake that was probably still sitting in the Professor's kitchen. Still I knew we had to keep going, and even if I had wanted to stop, and grab some berries off of a tree, Jimmy would have reminded me about saving the world, and all that junk. Oh, and how they might be poisonous.

Almost there, Jimmy stopped all of the sudden. He circled back a little bit.

"What are ya' doing…" I stopped too.

Then he ran over to a tree with some red berries on it, and started picking them off.

"This ain't no time to eat," I yelled at him, 'cause I was a little mad at him stealing my idea, but he kept picking them. "They might be poison, ya' know that genius?"

He was breathing too heavy to speak, so he showed me what he had in mind. With his hand he crushed the berries, so that the juices poured from between his fingers.

"You're making blood," I caught onto that really fast. He just bobbed his head, and tried to swallow down more air. I guess he had a choice of breathing or talking, and he chose breathing.

"Too light," I told him looking at the stream of berry juice dripping down his arm. Then he knelt down real quick, picked up a pinch of dirt, and mixed it with the berry juice. After a second the light red juice turned thicker and darker.

"Perfect," I told him, and it was. Jimmy had made perfect blood. Now if only everything else turned out this good. The black van would be coming along any second. So far we were two tired kids, with some fake blood, and beat up briefcase. Now it was onto Plan B.

CHAPTER 17. A BOY'S GOTTA DO, WHAT A BOY'S GOTTA DO

When we got to the place where the van would pass by we both were pretty winded. We could hear the car motor coming down the road already. There was no time to talk over our plan anymore. It was the time for action. I really wish we had had more time to work things out, especially since I wasn't totally sure what the plan was, or how Jimmy had gotten me involved again, or at least had had a little more time to back out of it altogether. We both had to do what we had to do, and hoped it worked out, and we didn't get shot. That to me was the most important part of the plan, not getting shot. Jimmy real quick like crushed the fake blood onto his chest and face. It didn't look too good with all the grease and dirt already on him. At first the berry juice had mixed in with the grease, and was hard to see, but it would have to do. Then he dove into the middle of the road, and laid face down. Kept really hoping they'd see him lying there in the cheesy pool of fake blood he had made. Probably not as much as Jimmy though, 'cause if they didn't see him, he'd be crushed under the van's wheels.

Me, I hid behind a tree right at the edge of the gravel, waited and kept my fingers crossed. Didn't have to wait too long. They showed up all too fast. In no time the van came zipping around the bend. "Please, let them see Jimmy;" I kept my eyes shut tight for a long time, and kept wishing. But then I remembered that I needed them open to do my part of the plan. The van was movin' kinda fast, faster than we thought they'd be coming. They got closer. Jimmy didn't move, not an inch, but I had to close my eyes again. Couldn't help myself. Still didn't hear the van stopping. Forced myself to open my eyes, 'cause I had to look again.

There was a loud screech. Geez, they almost didn't see him in time, but my boy Jimmy didn't twitch. Don't know if I could've laid there like that with that van speeding towards me. Guessing if he did it, I could have.

Anyway, it was the stop the stagecoach with the fallen log trick. They use to use that in the old cowboy movies, when the bad guys were planning on robbing the stagecoach. We didn't have a big log, so Jimmy's body seemed like the next best thing. It had worked. The guy behind the wheel jumped out of the front seat, and ran over to where Jimmy was lying in the middle of the road.

"It's the kid from the lab," he yelled to the other guy, who was still looking out through the windshield.

While that other guy was just watching what was going on, I made my move. Didn't have to think too much about it, danger was really my business again, and I still wasn't enjoying it much. Guess that's sort of the way James Bond felt about it, it was just a job, and you had to do it even if you didn't like it.

Moving fast, but light on my feet it wasn't easy, 'cause I was still carrying the briefcase. Real quick like I ducked down, and hid behind the van. Sat on the briefcase, and there right in front of me was the fishing line that Jimmy had pushed through the small opening in the van window. A thin piece of string that they probably didn't even take notice of as they left the lab. It was attached to a wire hook that Jimmy was able to catch onto the door lock. Good, I thought, one tug on that should open the tailgate. Hoped so anyway. What we wanted was for both of those guys to get out of the van, and check on Jimmy. But one of them was still sitting in the front seat on the passenger side.

"Come on, get out," I said to myself, but so far it was a no go.

"There's blood all over this kid," the one outside called back to his partner. He must've rolled Jimmy over.

"Is he still breathing?" came the answer.

Get out! Get out! Those were the words screaming out inside my head. I was still hoping.

"Do you think this was the work of that crazy kid who was screaming at the rabbits, nut case!" I guess being crazy was gonna be my defense when they dragged us into to court.

"Help me get him into the van!"

"What about our cargo?" the other guy asked.

"We'll drop him off at a hospital. One of us will stay with the van."

Good! Good! Still inside my head a voice was coaxing him on.

You could hear the van's door open. My hands tightened around the fishing line. I was finding it hard to breathe, and my body was shaking, as I was getting ready to pull it.

The guy left the door open, and began to walk over to Jimmy. I listened for their voices.

"What's wrong, where's he bleeding from?"

"Can't seem to find any injury. Maybe under this dirt..."

"No time now, let's get him to the van."

There was no time to waste for me either. Gave a good hard tug on the string. "Owww," it cut my hand. And it had hurt just enough for me get noticed.

"You hear something?" I heard one of them say.

Please, don't let them say yes, please don't say yes. I was talking to myself a lot that day.

"No, but with the cargo we're carrying in the back, we shouldn't spend too much time in the open like this."

"Let's get the kid in the van."

Pulled again on the string, this time easier, still nothing happened. I kept waiting for the click of the lock opening, but nothing. The motor revved. Smoke from the exhaust pipe blew into my face. In a second they'd be gone. Jimmy was inside. Didn't know what he could do. Had one chance. Made sure the wheels on the briefcase were locked in tight and right. Put my feet on it, crouched down, and grabbed hold of the bumper. The van began to move.

This ride was bumpy. We were still on the gravel road. Remember the wheels didn't run too well on bumpy roads. I was scared, and bouncing all over the place, waiting for the briefcase and me to tip over. One bump jolted me. Shot me upwards, but my feet somehow stayed with the briefcase. Don't know how much longer I could hold on. Just glad the van was moving slow now. One more jolt, the bumper cut into my fingers. Didn't even know what good me being there was doing. Just knew my best pal was in that van, and he might need help soon. Didn't know how much help I'd be, me skating, and holding on for my life on the top of worn out briefcase with wheels, but I wanted to be there just the same.

Real soon, we pulled out onto the regular road. The ride became a lot smoother now. That was the good news. The bad news was, the van started picking up speed. Now I was afraid to leave go. Lucky for me the wheels stayed locked in tight as we sped along. Left one hand loose to try and grab hold of the fishing line, but now it was blowing in the wind, and flying all over the place. It was high above my head one minute, then off to the other side of the van the next. Was afraid to reach too far for it. At the speed we were moving, I wanted to stay as close to the ground as possible, and hoped for no fast stops. Keeping my fingers crossed was not too easy right then.

The wind and the exhaust fumes were hitting me right in the face. Could hardly keep my eyes opened. All I could see was that string blowing around, just daring me to grab hold of it.

So far, we hadn't run into any traffic, and that was good. Kept waiting for a state trooper to pull me over for speeding. Finally, I dared to sneak a look in through the window. Real easy like, my legs pushed me up, and I could see the two Gravity Boxes covered with tarps.

Leaning against the side door was Jimmy. His head was lying on the seat, and you could tell that he was in his thinking mode. I could tell, 'cause that's all he ever did. Wanted him to look at me real bad, but couldn't think how I could get him to do that. You know, without letting those other guys know I was there along for the ride. Lucky, all at once I could see Jimmy's eyes rolling back and forth at the boxes. He still didn't know I was there. Probably thought I got ditched back in the woods. Would have waved my other hand, but standing like I was, leaving go at all was out of the question.

Then he saw me. His eyes almost bugged out of his head. Thought he was gonna give me away with a scream, or something, but he held back on that. Good going Jimmy, I thought. Had to duck down again to get my balance better, and to keep the guy who was driving from catching me in the rearview mirror. Jimmy was the thinker, but he couldn't have ridden this thing this far. Don't know how I was doing it. Didn't want to think too much about that. I had learned a long time ago, that thinking just got in the way when you were doing crazy stuff. Just kept my butt tucked in, and prayed I'd still have it tomorrow.

All at once we were joined by other traffic. Just came out of nowhere. Cars were zooming by in both directions, and now I was getting strange looks from old ladies in their Ford Pinto's, and little kids strapped in the backseat of their hatchbacks. There were others blasting horns, and some catching the attention of the agents driving the van, but that's not what bothered me. Coming on fast from behind were a set of flashing lights, and a siren blasting. Now I had to act with super speed, or it was all over.

Had maybe another minute before the G. Men knew that the siren was for them, and pulled over to the side of the road. Took a chance, and looked behind me real quick, the flashing lights were coming up on us fast, too fast. There was only one thing to do. Had to try to pull on the string one more time. What else could I do?

I kept wishing it would blow down to me. So far wishing hadn't made it happen. Had to let go with one hand again, then try to stand up on the briefcase, that was now sailing down the road at close to sixty miles an hour. Which I think was the land speed record for a

252

briefcase. Without me wanting it to, the case started to change directions swerving out to the side of the van. Almost lost my footing. The siren was getting louder. The second time I reached up with just my arm, but kept my chest tucked into my knees. The darn string kept breezing by my fingers. Could feel it brush by my hand, but could not get hold of it. The siren and lights were too close now, almost on top of us. Good, the van hadn't started slowing down yet. Had to give it my best shot, all I had. With a quick reach up, just keeping the one hand on the bumper, I swatted at the string with the other. The strong breeze sent it sliding through my fingers, and I closed them as fast as I could. With all my might I tugged down, there was a loud click, and the tale gate flung down. Just missed banging me in the head, and tossing me off of the back. The hatch was wide open. Only problem was now instead of the bumper to hold onto, all I had was fishing line that was ripping my hands apart. It really was scary now, something like water skiing with a wide mouthed shark right in front of you.

"What the…" One of the G. Men turned and yelled. Jimmy was right on top of the situation. Springing up from the pool of berry juice and grease, he had leaped over the seat, pulled the tarp away, and had already grabbed himself the closest Gravity Box. That was good for him, but old Shawn was about to play bumping cars with the oncoming traffic. The driver had started to step on the brakes, and I was now sailing into the back of the van. Just incase you didn't know, this briefcase didn't have any brakes. The siren right behind me was now the last thing on my mind, as I was about to have a head on collision with the tailgate.

Just before I rammed into the back of the van, a green beam shot out from underneath the tarp, and sent me sailing over the car. Thank you Jimmy, thanks Gravity Box! Made a perfect landing right in front of the van. Rolled about thirty feet when the case slowed to a halt. The green beam was gone, and Jimmy was still in the back of the van.

The van now skidded to a complete stop. The state trooper was pulling up alongside of it. Me, I jumped off of the case, and started running back to the van. First I had to run a few feet the other direction until I could slow down enough to turn around. In no time flat the two G. Men had jumped out of their front seats, and had pulled out their guns.

"Hold it right there," the command came, and I held it right there. Wasn't a G. Man though, it was the trooper, and he was pointing his own gun, a shotgun right at the both of the G Men. The two agents started to turn fast, but slowed down when they saw the barrel of the shotgun aimed right at them.

"I said hold it," the trooper screamed.

"You don't understand," one of the agents tried to get out.

"Drop those weapons," the trooper shouted, and ducked behind the door of the patrol car.

"We're government agents!"

"Well, if you don't put those weapons down, you'll never get a chance to prove it, will you?"

Real slow like the agents began to put their guns down on the ground.

"Just don't let those boys go anywhere."

"Right now, I'm not too worried about two boys," the trooper said, moving out real slow from behind the car door.

"Just don't..."

"You boys," the trooper meant the G. Men, "have some identification?" They started to put their hands in their pockets. "Nice and easy now!"

As the trooper was about to check out the agent's badges and ID's, a humming sound came traveling into my ear. Through the window of the van I could see Jimmy looking back at me. He knew what it was too, it was the chopper. It must have already dropped the Professor off at the hospital, and had come looking for the van. That fast the trooper had seen the ID's of the agents, and believed their story. In no time one agent was headed after me, and the other agent and the trooper were going after Jimmy.

"Don't move or I'll shoot," the trooper yelled out. It seemed like this guy was ready and willing to shoot anybody that day.

That goofball Jimmy was frozen. After all we'd been through he was frozen by a little shotgun. Me, I started to run, and then decided to do the thinking. About time, huh?

"I said I'll shoot," the trooper called out again. I guess that second warning was for me.

I guess a shotgun could throw a little scare into any of us. My legs halted like they were stuck into the ground. But my brain was still running at full speed, so I called back to Jimmy.

"Who's the most powerful kid in the universe?" Jimmy turned back to me. The trooper looked at me like I was crazy. The one agent was almost in the van, and one was almost on me. Tried again, even louder, "WHO'S THE MOST POWERFUL KID IN THE UNIVERSE?" Didn't know if it was gonna work. Jimmy just had to remember who was really in charge right there and then. One guy was just about to stick his head in the back of the van, when Jimmy shouted, "I AM... I AM THE MOST POWERFUL KID IN THE UNIVERSE!"

Just the words I wanted to hear. The green beam blasted the agent and the trooper about thirty feet back. Thought they were gonna smash into the police car, but it landed them nice and soft on top of it, and didn't even make a scratch in the paint. The other guy grabbed me, but Jimmy was now free to get out of there.

"It's all over kid," the agent said as he held me around the neck.

The chopper was moving in closer. The inside of the van glowed bright green, and Jimmy zoomed out of the back, and through the air like he was wearing a jetpack.

"Bring it back kid! Bring it back," said the agent squeezing tighter around my neck. For a minute Jimmy looked confused, as he circled back to look at us. So, I can't really say if it was Jimmy or the box that did what happened next. Anyway, the next flash of green sent both the agent and me shooting into the sky. You could tell this guy wasn't use to flying on his own, 'cause he almost strangled me trying not to let go.

The chopper was just hovering over us, like they didn't know what to expect next. I know I didn't. A second beam shot back to the van, and lifted the other box right up to where the guy was holding me.

256

"Let go of him," Jimmy ordered. He was being kinda' pushy now, 'cause I think he liked taking charge. Gee it was neat bossing grown-ups around.

"What are you trying to do kid," my agent was getting a little of his courage back.

"Just leave him go!"

"Do you know what you're doing?"

"Leave him go," Jimmy had a one-track mind, and for the first time I was really glad about that.

"Who do you think you are kid?" This could've gone on for hours.

"I'm the most powerful kid in the universe," and Jimmy said it like he really meant it.

Good answer, but it looked like it was a no go. The agent had me, and there was no way he was gonna let me go.

Suddenly, the beam seemed to let go of him. Now it was only holding me up. Then Jimmy, or the beam brought us up even higher. When the G Man started to feel the beam losing its grip on him, he began to slide down my body. His fingers clenched tight into my shoulders. It was hurting in fact. He now had his legs wrapped tight around my legs, just trying not to fall. I was kinda skinny, so there wasn't gonna be much to hang on to. Me being all covered in grease wasn't making it much easier for this guy. Still he held tight.

There was a lot of traffic starting to gather around us now. People were slowing down, trying to figure what the heck was going on. The trooper still had his shotgun drawn, and the agent on the ground was starting to go for his own weapon again. The side window

257

on the helicopter slid open, and the muzzle of some kinda machine gun stuck out of it. Think it was pointing right at Jimmy. If he was shot we'd all crash. Just like the foreign spies, I guess these agents didn't care about their own guys either. This time they weren't gonna talk to us. They knew Jimmy could stop them too easy with the Gravity Box. So I think they were planning on shooting us down. Just that fast two more beams shot out of the box Jimmy was holding. Both purple, one that bounced off of the agent holding me, and the other rocketed straight up into the air. Whatever it was, it made everyone just stop to watch. The beam that hit the guy on my back must've been to make him heavier, 'cause he couldn't hold on anymore. He just slid on down me like a fireman down a fire pole. Almost took my pants with him.

The second purple light had struck a cloud straight overhead. That fast it had started to fall to the ground. Don't know what everybody thinks a cloud can do if it hits you, but they were all starting to scream and scramble out of the way, the cars, the chopper, everyone was running for their lives. Might think it weighed a million pounds the way everyone was diving for cover. I'd already been hit by a cloud once today, so I knew not to worry.

Jimmy sent out another beam from his machine, and the second Gravity Box now floated right over to me like a friendly pup. Just before he could touch down, I saw the falling agent make a nice soft landing on top of the van. He might have made a little dent. The cloud now covered everything, and it seemed like fog was everywhere. The chopper had disappeared in the dark, gray mist, and all we could see was the cloud swirling around and around where the

258

chopper was. Now no one could see anything. The giant cloud just parked itself on the ground, so that everything had to stop down there too.

"Over here," Jimmy called, and I followed the sound of his voice. Found him pretty fast too.

"Where's the briefcase?" he asked me.

"What do ya want that for?" After all we were the baddest dudes in the universe, so I didn't see how a water pistols filled with ink and fishing line were gonna be of any use to us. Although, I was pretty sure after we destroyed the Gravity Boxes, we'd be the two saddest dudes in the universe, or at lease on this planet.

"Got an idea!"

"Ah, I remember, I remember where it is!"

"Then just imagine it up here."

Could hardly see the beam cutting through the cloud, and lifting the briefcase up to us.

"We're outlaws now," I said.

"Maybe not, come on!" He took off, and I stayed close enough that I could follow him right through the top of the cloud.

Jimmy tried telling me what we were gonna do, but the noise of the chopper wasn't far behind. It was making it really hard to hear. Like a second later it pulled up out of the fog. They were hot on our trail, and our trail was taking us right to the other side of town. The chopper was staying close, but not too close. Me and Jimmy kept zigzagging, so it'd be hard to shoot at us. We let them stay on top of us for so long, and then going with the plan, we zipped way ahead of them. They still were following, and they picked up their speed too.

Suddenly other choppers surrounded us. They began trying to circle us. But they couldn't move as well or as fast as we could. Right then it seemed like the whole army was coming after us.

"We could lose these guys easy," I yelled to Jimmy.

"Stick to the plan," he screamed back at me.

And it didn't seem like we had much choice, what with more than ten choppers beginning to crowd our air space. I was hoping that the Gravity Boxes didn't get a mind of their own again, and try and shoot them down. But as long as the choppers weren't firing on us the boxes stayed well behaved, and did just what they were told.

In no time there seemed to be ground support moving in on us. Out of nowhere several black cars arrived on the scene. They were beeping their horns, flashing their lights, and sirens were blasting as they moved in and out of traffic trying to follow the choppers and us. At that end of town there was no more fog on the ground, and now it was just as easy for them to see us as us to see them. And they had it all covered. I guess that's how important the boxes were, but still no one fired, probably afraid of hurting the Gravity Boxes. Me and Jimmy just zipped through the clouds, and kept just enough distance between us, so that they couldn't catch up. At this point, I think they were as scared as we were. After all Jimmy had told them exactly who they were dealing with.

Suddenly we speeded up moving straight ahead, and it was only us and the choppers. In no time we were right above our target area, the town trash incinerator. It was getting late in the day, and it seemed empty of people. That was really good for us, and Jimmy's plan. People could've messed up everything. All at once we took a quick nosedive down. One of the choppers was only about a minute behind.

Just as they were about to land there was a loud explosion, and then another loud explosion. The fire had blown out of the furnace, and the smoke from the blast was filling up the air. Me and Jimmy were choking on the fumes, and it looked like an angry volcano had erupted all around us. And it was almost as hard to see then, as it was when the cloud had fallen down to the ground back on the highway.

The chopper touched down right after. The first man out didn't even stop to look at us, but ran right over to check out the fire. After only minute of staring down in total disbelief, he turned to look at us.

"Do you two know what you've done?"

I couldn't answer, even though I had a real good idea what we had just done. Jimmy couldn't answer either, even if he had wanted to. In seconds all of the men from the chopper surrounded us. Still we didn't say anything, and I think that was the best answer we could have given them.

"Do you know what the punishment is for the theft and destruction of government property?" another one said.

The smoke had begun to clear up, but it still burned my eyes. So maybe it was the heat and cinders in the air that made my eyes tear. That's the story I was going with anyway. Turned my head to look at Jimmy, hoping his head was down, and he was thinking, but it was a no go on the thinking. Instead he was looking right up at the agent, who had just talked to us.

"Do you know?" the same guy yelled at us again.

That's when Jimmy cleared his throat, and I hoped what he was gonna say wasn't gonna get us into more trouble.

"Excuse me sir, but who stole it first?"

"What?"

"You stole them first, we just stole it back, and did what the Professor wanted us to do with them."

"The Professor, he was in on this?"

"Don't think this will make him unhappy," Jimmy said back to him.

"He wasn't really sick either, was he?"

Jimmy didn't answer his question but said; "you really shouldn't make him go on the helicopter, the Professor's afraid of heights, you know."

There was now a long staring contest between him and Jimmy. I was too afraid to stare, so I just looked at the ground, and tried to look innocent. I had gotten a lot of practice doing that with my parents. Was hoping if any hitting went on, it would be all on Jimmy for opening his big yap. Right then I was just happy being the quiet, stupid one.

One agent turned to another, "any chance of retrieving anything?"

"What is there to retrieve," the guy who seemed to be in charge yelled at him, and then he tried to get hold of his temper. "The machines exploded when they hit the flames. By the time we'd turn down the heat enough to even go near it, even the metal scraps would be melted. No chance!"

"We should take them in," another agent said.

The guy who seemed to be in charge, stopped, and seemed to be thinking about it for a minute.

"You saw what that thing could do," he said.

Then there was a quiet moment when nobody spoke. The agent looked back at me and Jimmy.

"You boys have both been briefed?"

"Yes sir," Jimmy said.

"What's that mean?" I tried to ask, 'cause I really didn't know.

"It means you'll keep your mouths shut about all of this," the guy screamed back in my face. "Listen I'm going on the carpet for this, and I am not a happy man here. Two punk kids," he shook his head like he couldn't believe none of it.

"Sorry," I said, and that only seemed to make him angrier.

"You will be visited by some of my people, and we will be keeping an eye on you, the both of you."

He waved to the other men who began walking back to the chopper. When he was there all alone with me and Jimmy, he spoke very softly to both of us.

"Any hands that the gravity machines would've fallen into would have been the wrong hands, but you boys better hope you never run into me again!" That's all he said, then he walked back to the chopper that he had come in, and it took off. As the choppers started to circle, we waved. We were starting to get cocky already.

"Were you crying Shawn?" Jimmy looked at me.

"No, it was a cinder or something" I hadn't actually cried.

When the helicopter was out of sight, we howled like a couple of wolves. We had gotten away with it, and we were home free, we hoped.

EPPI-LOG

Eppi-log. Jimmy told me that that means the end of the story, or something like that. Or what happens after the end of the story. And then I said to him: "Isn't the end of the story when it's really over." I mean, when you think about it, how can anything really happen after the story is over. He just looked at me like he wanted to hit me or something, so I just shut my trap. But somehow, we had gotten to the end of the story, and here's what happened after that.

The Professor naturally recovered. Since he wasn't really sick that was easy enough, and I'm sure you would have guessed it just the same.

We became big heroes to our parents, but were under strict orders not to let anybody else know just how great we were. Ricky was a big hero too. But all it took was a bone and bowl of milk to shut his trap. They were just happy to have us back home, so stealing the Gravity Boxes was something we didn't talk too much about.

That night I took a good hot bath. Felt good too, to get all that slime off of me. Ate good, and went to bed. Went there just long enough to let my parents think I was in for the night. Was too excited to sleep anyway. It was Jimmy's idea to fake going to bed. He knew we'd never be allowed out without proper rest, and at that time of night, but as you know a secret agent's work is never done. There was just one more thing left to do.

I sneaked out, and met Jimmy down the corner from my house. It was late, but we were getting use to the hours. From there we cut through some back yards, and headed towards the edge of town. We didn't want to run into anybody. Got there in about twenty minutes. It was rough getting around on foot and on the ground.

Although the incinerator ran all night, the high cyclone fence was closed. Guess it cost too much to keep starting it up, and turning it off.

I was over easy, being the best climber. Jimmy was right behind me though. We were back for what we had left there earlier. Way in the back of some big stacks of rubble that were waiting to be burned was some smaller clumps of junk. We dug in quietly, so that nobody would hear us. With the loud crackling and thunder from the furnace we didn't think that anyone could, but why chance it? We had come so close, no need to botch things now. For a second we weren't sure we'd found the right place, but then I felt one of the handles. Real easy like I dragged out one of the Gravity Boxes from under the pile junk.

"Shhh…" Jimmy told me as some trash fell off to the side.

"Lucky for us," I said.

"Lucky for the world," Jimmy said.

You see that's why we needed the briefcase. There was just enough powder to make two more nice explosions. They were beautiful too. Had to time it perfectly, so that the guys in the choppers would get there just in time to see it. While Jimmy was putting together the Ultra Counterintelligence Incendiary Device, you guessed it again, Number 9 out of his briefcase, and out of a large tomato can we found, I was busy hiding the boxes. Pretty neat huh?

The explosions Jimmy made were not very big. Don't know what he expected with the little bit of powder he had left, so just before I had buried the second Gravity Box under the mountain of trash, I grabbed hold of the handles. Right then I imagined the green beam of light blasting some of the trash near the incinerator high into the sky. It looked great too. With all the dust and smoke it had made, it looked like we had dropped a giant bomb into the fire. Guess with the sound of the chopper whizzing around, the fact that Jimmy's Ultra Device Number 9 didn't make that much noise didn't matter. Jimmy jumped a little when the beam sent everything flying high into the air. Then he looked at me, smiled, and gave me a big thumbs up sign. Anyway, it looked like a really big explosion, and was enough to fool anyone who saw it.

If we had been arrested, the guys who worked at the junkyard would have probably incinerated the boxes along with a bunch of other junk that they were hid with. That's why Jimmy called this plan his "fail safe system." No matter what, the agents still wouldn't have gotten their hands on the boxes. Anyway, that's the way we had hoped it would work out. But for now, all we wanted to do was have a little fun. As long as nobody found out, what harm could it do? I mean we weren't planning to take over the world. Not yet anyway. Ha! Ha!

"Up, up, and away," Jimmy said, and as he took to the sky, I followed his lead. Real nice like we soared up and over the town, just above the clouds, so nobody could see us, just two kids out for a joy

267

ride. Later we might destroy the Gravity Boxes like the Professor wanted. Who knows? Now we were just having some kicks. But I think the most important thing we learned from playing with the Gravity Boxes, is that if we could imagine it we could make it happen. Kinda like life, I guess. So, if you think about it, what was wrong with the two most powerful kids in the universe having some fun?

THE END

www.ingramcontent.com/pod-product-compliance
Lightning Source LLC
Chambersburg PA
CBHW051540260626
47170CB00003B/1028